Dear Reader,

Do *you* have a secret fantasy? Everybody does.
Maybe it's to be rich and famous and beautiful. Or to
start a no-strings affair with a sexy mysterious stranger.
Or to have a sizzling second chance with a former
sweetheart.... You'll find these dreams—and much
more—in Temptation's exciting new yearlong
promotion, Secret Fantasies.

Imaginative Regan Forest contributes this month's story.
At night, small-town waitress Ellen Montrose dreams of
the Whitfield mansion, of dancing in the ballroom with a
handsome stranger. But fantasy and reality collide when
he mysteriously arrives in town—in the flesh.

In the coming months, look for Secret Fantasies books by
Lynn Michaels, Kate Hoffmann and Tiffany White. Please
write and let us know how you enjoy the "fantasy."

Happy Reading!

The Editors

c/o Harlequin Temptation
225 Duncan Mill Road
Don Mills, Ontario
M3B 3K9
Canada

Dear Reader,

The idea for *The Man from Shadow Valley* began
with my fascination over actual accounts of people
who share identical dreams. Lovers meeting on the
dreamscape? What a start for a romance novel!

And where better to set the story than in a deserted
mansion? As a child, I gazed up at such a house,
picturing ghosts from the past and wondering who
the people were that lived there....

In grade school my friends found out I walked home
with a classmate, Ethel, who lived on the poor side of
town. I can still recall their stinging taunts today.
What could that little girl have felt? She, too, must
have gazed at mansions, weaving secret fantasies of her
own. Ethel was my inspiration for Ellen, who conquers
her past.

Life has its strange twists. Recently I moved to the
country, and on a road not far away—standing high on
a hill—is an old abandoned house. It is surrounded only
by silence as its white paint chips away. Every time I
drive by, I become Ellen in Shadow Valley, dreaming.
Except that she dreamed of fantasy gowns to draw and
I dream of fantasy stories to write.

As a writer, sharing wild and mysterious fantasies with
readers is such a special privilege! What more could
any dreamer ask for?

Sincerely,

Regan Forest

Cody Laird is back in town

Back to Shadow Valley. Back to Pebble Street.

Only now, he has a new name. He's successful—
he just bought the town's radio station. Nobody
remembers him as the poor boy from the wrong
side of the tracks. Everyone in Shadow Valley
wants to know him.

Everyone except Ellen Montrose—the one
woman he wants, needs and desires. Ellen and
his dreams of her are what pulled him back to
Shadow Valley. Cody's plans include a future
with Ellen.

But Ellen's don't.

The Man from Shadow Valley is **Regan Forest's** thirteenth Temptation novel—and what better number to have as part of the Secret Fantasies miniseries? This popular author recently moved to southern Indiana, to the country, and loves being surrounded by woods, meadows and water. "It's beautiful," Regan declares. "I've dreamed about living in the country for years, and the reality is even better." The only thing missing in this idyllic existence is a dog, which she and her husband plan to adopt soon.

Books by Regan Forest

HARLEQUIN TEMPTATION
226—HEAVEN SENT
311—HIDDEN MESSAGES
355—THE LADY AND THE DRAGON
399—SECRET LIVES
418—BORROWED TIME
464—THE SHERIFF OF DEVIL'S FORK

THE MAN FROM SHADOW VALLEY

REGAN FOREST

Harlequin Books

TORONTO • NEW YORK • LONDON
AMSTERDAM • PARIS • SYDNEY • HAMBURG
STOCKHOLM • ATHENS • TOKYO • MILAN
MADRID • WARSAW • BUDAPEST • AUCKLAND

For Kathy Burns

ISBN 0-373-25638-8

THE MAN FROM SHADOW VALLEY

Prologue

ELLEN WAS NINE when she first saw the ghost.

It was twilight. Uneasy shadows prowled the gloom of Pebble Street. As always, the last hovering light of day stirred up discontent like dust before it settled under cover of night. Twilight—a time to run.

A ball game was going on in the weed-grown vacant lot. Shouts of children carried on the summer breeze toward the weathered, unpainted porches where adults sat swatting at flies and drinking beer. None turned to look at the barefoot child who trotted past them down the length of the dirty street.

There was a field beyond the last house, where carcasses of mining trucks lay rusting under thistle grass and gnarled weeds. Spiders lived in those steel corpses; Ellen wouldn't go near them. She hurried by, and rushed even faster past the cemetery—a place of grim, battered headstones and haunted shadows. Forsaken souls lived there. Above rose the slope with violet-blue bruises and claw marks where mine buildings had once stood. Crickets hissed cheerless tunes and tree frogs snarled at the setting sun. Finally, she reached a lane overhung with giant cottonwoods. Excitement grew; her heart beat faster and she picked up speed until she reached a circle of chokecherry bushes and wild roses. Her secret place.

Ellen stopped abruptly, out of breath. Just across the lane was a locked iron gate. Above it, against clear pink sky, stood

a mansion on the hill. The late sun's rays splashed a thin net-
ting of gold over the mansion, a sheeny veil of magic. If she
stood still and listened, she could hear the music of the breezes
that sang around its chimneys and gables.

When darkness began to fall and the sweet perfume of
honeysuckle rose in the air, Ellen sat down on a mossy log to
watch the lights come on.

They came on in the sky first. Diamonds twinkling and
laughing and teasing the high, high roof with magic sparkles. The house could touch the stars when it wished to.
Then, soon, in the lower windows, lights began to glow, one
by one.

The topmost windows remained dark. People said the third
floor was a ballroom, unused for decades. Ellen fixed her eyes
on the dark windows, imagining a room lit by crystal span-
gles where couples waltzed to the music of violins, the women
in flowing gowns and satin slippers, with diamonds sparkling at their throats....

Then suddenly *it* was there! A frosty light moving through
the tendrils of night, glowing in the third-story windows! Ellen shuddered with an ice-cold thrill. The ghost—luminous
and floating across the dark and empty ballroom!

After that night, she saw it often, but the ghost wasn't why
she came. It was the mansion itself that drew her. Each sight
of it lit the flame of another of her dreams. Someday, she, too,
would live in a house like this!

ALTHOUGH IT WAS CALLED the Whitfield mansion, Ellen knew
it was inhabited by an elderly couple named Mr. and Mrs.
Meullar. The summer she turned eleven, there was talk
around Shadow Valley that their granddaughter had come
to visit, and at a band concert in the park, Ellen saw her—a
girl her own age wearing a yellow voile dress and matching
yellow shoes and carrying a white purse. She looked like a

princess. The barefoot girls from Pebble Street made fun of the frilly dress to hide their pangs of envy. For Ellen, the envy was agonizing. Not as much for the dress, as for the fact that this girl got to be *inside* the mansion. She actually slept there, and could climb the stairways and explore the magnificent rooms.

That girl, Carolyn, never returned to Shadow Valley. Rumors spread that she had told stories of an evil spirit in the house, a terrifying ghost who never rested.

I have seen it! Ellen thought. *I have seen the ghost!*

During those endless childhood years of secondhand clothes and cruel glances, she went often to the gate to gaze up at the magnificent house, and escape into her daydreams. Someday *she* would live in a mansion. She would sit in exquisite rooms dressed in blue velvet, and serve guests from a silver tea service. She would light the ballroom with a thousand candles and dance in glimmering gowns of lace and satin. There would be parties. And there would always be music.

Someday...

1

ONE EVENING IN THE summer of her twenty-fourth year, Ellen Montrose stood at the bottom of the hill, looking up at the Whitfield mansion that stood silent and dying against a lonely sky. A For Sale sign at the gate was rusted by rain and bent by wind, the name of its Denver real-estate firm now barely discernible. Carolyn Meullar, the owner, hadn't been seen near the mansion for years; she only wanted to be rid of it.

To be rid of it. The thought pulled at Ellen's heart and caused her eyes to mist. The house on the hill was a living thing, with a soul hurt by secrets and horrors and dead dreams, and no one cared about its pain but her.

Tears turned the sun's glow to haze, like the mysterious mist from days past, when the mansion's enchantment had lured her. Ellen still came, but not often. She still longed to see the inside, because in her imaginary pictures of its majestic interior, a million childhood dreams had sprouted, and her lifelong goals had taken root. The mansion had given purpose to her life. Even now, languishing in slow decay, it was still her inspiration.

Why she chose to walk out to the hill this day, Ellen couldn't say, unless somehow the lonely ghost of Whitfield had summoned her. Just to remind her of her dreams.

That night, from the silent depths of the mansion, the ghost invaded her sleep.

Ellen entered a pink-and-gold foyer with gilded mirrors and crystal vases filled with flowers. French doors opened on each side and a wide staircase rose, winding up into dusky sprays of light—moonlight from a high window. She stared up into the stairwell. Something was up there!

The front door swung shut, trapping her inside. A sound of ghostly moaning moved through the darkness from some discarnate soul wandering lost. Ellen gasped in fear. Shivers coursed along her spine. She froze to the one spot on the marble landing.

Shadows trembled under the frosty light from the high window over the twisting stairway and suddenly a figure stepped into the haze. Ellen drew another startled breath, too frightened to run. But as her focus sharpened, the figure became a man, not a ghost. Moonlight illuminated his handsome face and beamed life into his gray eyes.

A soft, unsure smile formed on his lips, as if her presence in the house was a surprise. She grasped the oak railing for support and took a step back. The man held out his hand, inviting her to come up the stairs.

Up into the uncertain darkness where the ghost lurked. Forlorn, tremulous moaning began to echo from the top of the house. Ellen gazed in confusion at the muscular arm and extended open hand. She had seen the hand before, seen the face before . . . but where? Who was he? What did he want? What was he doing in her mansion?

Behind her, from somewhere in the deep gloom, came the ghostly moans again. The young man advanced down a step, again extending his hand, as if to offer her an escape from the danger. Hesitantly, Ellen reached out.

His strong grasp assuaged her fear. Yet he wanted to entice her up there to the high rooms where greater danger lurked. Surrounded by fear, even of him, Ellen resisted. When she did so, the grip of his hand loosened and the marble tiles began to sway and dissolve under her feet . . . and he disappeared as *suddenly as he had come. She stood alone, caged in darkness.*

Ellen shook herself awake. *Crazy dream.* Served her right for walking out by the Whitfield mansion in the afternoon. That man, that severely handsome man... How had her imagination conjured *him* up?

A full moon shone into her window. No wonder her sleep was restless tonight; the full moon always tugged at her like it pulled the tides. Her eyes fluttered open. It wasn't the moon; sunshine was streaming through her east window. In the slow afterglow of the dream, she yawned, smiling. How beautiful the mansion was! Such a jolting contrast to the despairing reality of this—her waking world.

Nine o'clock. Outside her open upstairs window, a dog was barking and neighborhood boys were playing noisily, shouting insults at each other. Tuning out the fight, she invited the songs of the summer birds into her consciousness. Overhanging branches of the oak tree beside the house were filled with chirping and warbling. Drawing back the thin lace curtains, Ellen looked out on the street of decaying homes— some boarded shut—and narrow lawns choked with weeds. In a yard directly across the street, dewdrops tried uselessly to brighten the rusted shells of old cars that had lain there for years.

Pebble Street. Wincing at the sight of it, Ellen closed her eyes and lifted her face toward the sun to take in its warmth and its promise.

Morning sunlight, golden beams,
Show me riches, show me dreams.
Sunlight, shine a path for me
Toward the place I'm meant to be.

Where the verse came from, she didn't know. Its words had formed a ritual since her childhood, as much a part of the morning as brushing her hair. On the bleakest winter day, with dawn no more than a pale glow in the east, her recitation was the same—a plea, and a reminder that somewhere in the world the sun was bright and warm and welcoming. Somewhere far from Shadow Valley.

Ellen slid into a pair of jeans and an oversize shirt and made her bed. On it she carefully spread out a square of fine white silk under a blouse pattern hand-cut from old Christmas tissue paper and began to work.

The cutting-out was finished by ten-thirty, when she had to be downstairs to fix a late breakfast for her grandfather. Tonight, if she managed to get home before midnight, some of the seams could get basted. If the project turned out as she expected, the design would be added to her portfolio and the finished blouse included in a wardrobe Shadow Valley would never see.

AT THE BLUE SPRUCE Truck Stop, a twangy country song floated over the rattle of dishes, gruff laughter, and the roar of an eighteen-wheeler pulling in. In the ladies' room, Ellen tied her starched organza apron over her black skirt, smoothed back her short blond hair with an antique herringbone clip, and straightened the strand of fake pearls at her neck.

In the dining area, a trucker in red plaid raised a mug in the air as soon as he saw her enter from the kitchen door. "Hey," he demanded with a grin. "More coffee!"

Ellen picked up a coffeepot from the warmer and made her way to his table. When the customer made a grab for the tie of her apron, she stepped back abruptly, spilling hot coffee on his hand. He howled in pain and jerked away.

A bearded trucker sitting nearby scolded, "Nobody touches the princess." He winked at her affectionately.

"Ah, our uppity Pebble Princess," the first man chimed in.

Ellen's eyes narrowed in mild contempt. She was used to this, but it was a lousy way to start her shift. "Pour it yourself, Altman." She set the pot on his table and walked away, head high, straightening the bow of her crisp white apron.

Never would she let on how the words burned. She was labeled for the street where she was born, the street where she lived. The street that strangled her in its dust and shame. The truck driver, Harvey Altman, was one of many who had taunted her in school when they were kids—he and his sister Nan, who laughed at her clothes—and he was still at it. From across the room, she glared at Altman. Someday she'd show him. Someday she'd show them all.

In her mind's eye her next creation took form—an elegant beige silk-crepe gown. Narrow skirt and slim bodice fashioned from the once-exquisite resale dress she'd found at a little shop in Golden. Ellen saw herself wearing her own high-style gown, moving like a model through a tuxedo-clad crowd....

But the vision was hard to preserve in the company of customers involved in racy dialogues of the road and a country singer on the radio loudly lamenting his last one-night stand. *Maybe,* she thought distractedly, *she should have held more tightly to the hand of the stranger in the dream. Wherever he meant to lead her would have been an improvement on this. She could have seen all of the mansion, at last, even with the meddlesome ghost after them. What could a ghost do, anyway?*

By the time Millie Miller arrived for her late-night shift, the sun had sunk well behind the mountains. Reflections of the red neon light blinked in the truck-stop windows. Millie, in her tight jeans, rushed in as her boyfriend's pickup roared away.

"The sky is all lit up with a full moon rising," Millie said, pushing up the sleeves of her sweatshirt and reaching for her short green-and-white-striped apron. "It's quiet enough in here, though."

"So far," Ellen answered. "Those drivers in the corner are loading up on coffee. They'll be leaving soon. Harvey Altman's in here for the second time tonight, probably got kicked out of the house by his wife. If he leaves a tip, you keep it. I'll take nothing from the likes of him."

Millie was tying back her long brown hair with a ribbon. "What'd he do? Call you Pebble Princess? They all do, so what? You're too damn sensitive."

"Maybe I am. But what gives these guys the right to talk to women like they do? How I choose to dress is none of their business."

"Ah, they're just stupid. Just because you wear pearls instead of jeans and you talk proper and won't accept any date offers, they assume you think you're too good for them."

"I *am* too good for them. I'm tired of being made fun of. I've been tired of it since I was three."

Ellen poured pepper, stifling a sneeze. Because there were few customers, she had gathered the salt-and-pepper shakers and lined them up on the counter for refills. Millie went to wait on a young couple just entering.

While the radio was playing a sad and bitter song, and Ellen was washing down the chipped orange countertop, the little bell on the door jingled to announce a customer. The man chose a booth in the corner. Because Millie had gone into the kitchen for a cigarette break, Ellen quickly dried her hands and picked up a plastic-covered menu.

But when she looked toward the booth, a rush of cold followed by a shiver of intense heat charged her senses. That man! He looked just like—

He was identical to the man in her dream; was even dressed the same, in jeans and a light-colored shirt with sleeves rolled up past the elbows. Dark hair with a slight windblown look, the way he had first appeared on the winding stairs out of the clots of darkness, as if moments earlier he had been hurrying from somewhere. Yet there was nothing in his demeanor, then or now, that hinted of haste, turbulence, or even distraction.

The heat that had begun vibrating through her body flamed in Ellen's cheeks. Stiff as a robot, she walked across the room and handed him the menu. The man looked up and smiled—exactly the same smile she had seen in her sleep. The ceiling lights caught the gray of his eyes and turned them blue. Her heart began to beat so hard she was afraid he could see the pounding through her blouse, and she involuntarily held her breath because in the dream he had seemed to know her.

But there was no sign of recognition in his eyes. Ellen smiled rigidly, trying unsuccessfully to release herself from anticipation of a drumroll or her name warbled from his lips. She scolded herself. What in the name of sanity did she expect?

Her own voice came out as a self-conscious squeak. "Hi."

"Hi," he answered casually, as if the planet were still in orbit and all the stars were still in the sky. "I don't need a menu. I just want coffee and a turkey sandwich."

"Toasted?"

"No, plain."

"French fries?

He shrugged. "Are they pretty good?"

"Yes, if the volume we sell is any indication."

Millie's voice boomed from behind her, "Translated, that means we got the best fries in Colorado. Ask any driver on the road."

"Okay, I'm convinced." He smiled again, his eyes fixed momentarily on Millie. "I didn't need a translation."

Ellen glanced sideways at the other waitress, who had come up silently and startled her. *Blast it, even Millie gave her a bad time about the way she talked.* Well, let them have their fun. When she left Shadow Valley, she would take no residue of a "white trash" label with her. Years of study to learn proper speech also required years of practice until it became second nature. Others resented her high-flung ambitions. Let them.

Without a word, she turned and headed for the kitchen to give the order to the cook. Normally, good manners would have dictated another pleasant smile flashed at the customer, but in the presence of this man, Ellen didn't trust her own reflexes. It was like coming face-to-face with a phantom!

He wasn't a trucker because his entry wasn't preceded by the sound of a big truck engine roaring in. He must be someone just traveling through. He would eat his sandwich and disappear, just as he had done in the dream. *No, just like someone who* looked *like him in the dream*, she corrected.

Some moments later, another man—Shadow Valley's youngest veterinarian—joined him. Dr. Jeff Calhoun occasionally came in during late hours when he had been out on emergency calls. That he would know the stranger baffled Ellen enough to wonder if she was still dreaming—dreaming all of this....

But the veterinarian was real enough. She set a steaming cup in front of the stranger while she greeted Dr. Calhoun. "Good evening. Will you have coffee, too?"

He nodded pleasantly. "Yeah, thanks, Ellen. No menu, just coffee and a large slice of lemon pie." He turned to his companion. "I recommend the pies here."

Minutes dragged by like tortured hours for Ellen. She studied the phantom of last night's dream from a distance, a few casual seconds at a time, trying not to stare. There *was* that vaguely familiar something about him. From the dream, of course. But how could she dream of a man she didn't know?

The mens' heads bent in conversation while they ate. It wasn't the body language of small talk. When she refilled their coffee cups, Ellen caught snippets about the music being played on the radio. Locals had been talking about the Shadow Valley station this past week because the programming had changed. Ellen hadn't given it much thought.

Business picked up as two regulars settled into the adjoining booth, waving for Ellen's attention. She approached with her usual forced smile. "Beef stew is the special tonight."

One trucker removed his hat, the other didn't. Ellen kept it to herself that she noticed such things. Her grandfather hadn't worn a hat indoors in his life; he considered it outrageously ill-mannered.

"You're looking pretty tonight," the hatless man said, grinning.

The other, whose name was Spence, chimed in, "Well, hey, did you ever see our Pebble Princess when she wasn't looking right spiffy?"

Anger shot into her like an arrow. Through years of practice, Ellen outwardly ignored the remark. Inwardly, she seethed. The dream look-alike, seated with the back of his head only inches from Spence, could not help but overhear. She detected a slight turn of his head and a pause in his conversation. Or at least it seemed so. Could his reaction be only her own paranoia kicking up? A stranger to Shadow Valley wasn't likely to know Pebble Street.

Something changed, though. She felt it. Or thought she felt it. Once, from across the room, he glanced up and met her eyes with an uninterpretable expression—mysteriously placid, even friendly. Ellen couldn't bring herself to look in his direction again.

By eleven o'clock the café was all but empty. Dr. Calhoun and the phantom had been gone over two hours, and Ellen was so dream-logged from the experience, every little sound and shadow made her jump. The stranger's face haunted her and his eyes seemed to be still watching her from some invisible place. It was a welcome relief when her shift was over at eleven-thirty.

Walking home through the town of Shadow Valley, Ellen felt last night's dreams creep up out of the shadows like serpents, evoking a strong sense of fear. Fear of a ghost. Fear of a coincidence that had no explanation.

The air smelled of flowers and pine trees, and the special magic of a Colorado mountain summer. But when she reached Pebble Street, the atmosphere of the July night changed. Brooding shadows skulked through the moonlight like dark mist clinging to the ground—shadows of poverty and despair and memories better forgotten. Even the night couldn't hide the personality of the street where she lived.

The porch light was on. Her grandfather never forgot to leave it on for her. Ellen hurried across the small stretch of lawn that the old man tended with care. Hollyhocks and iris bloomed along the walk—the only flowers on the street except for those few that grew untended year after year along the alley.

The front door squeaked when she closed it behind her. Softly, she made her way to her grandfather's bedroom, as she always did, to check on him. The old man slept peacefully with his eyeglasses on the bed beside an open book. He was reading *Look Homeward, Angel* again. Ellen's heart filled with love. Smiling, she picked up the book, placed the marker, and set it with his glasses on the bedside table next to his pipe.

Her grandfather was the only reason she stayed. Without her, he would be alone in his last years. She didn't resent him for keeping her home, because as a girl Ellen had needed him and he had always been there. Now he needed her—needed her love and her care. Lately, he had not been well.

In the upstairs room that had been the master bedroom when her grandmother was alive, she hand-basted the silk blouse, trying hard to concentrate. Each minute that passed distanced the events of the evening further, making them seem less real, so it became easier to try to convince herself the resemblance between the man in her dream and tonight's stranger was the work of her overactive imagination. Her head was eager to accept the theory; her heart was far more stubborn.

Sometime after two she went to bed and closed her eyes against the haunting residue of the puzzle, and the dream came drifting in....

The dust smelled like a fearful memory. No one had been in this splendorous room for a very long time. Crystal chandeliers overhead were laced with cobwebs; none were lighted. Through gray gloom came the echo of a deep, velvet soft masculine voice. "Ellen? Where are you?"

She knew the voice from somewhere—perhaps from long ago. Turning around and around in the moonlit room, she searched for him. No moving shadow announced him this time; he materialized beside her as if he had been there all the time and she simply had not seen....

She knew him now; knew the soft sheen of his dark brown hair, and the intensity of his powder gray eyes. She knew him—but who was he?

"I've been waiting for you," he said. "I knew you'd come back."

"Why am I here?" she asked, bewildered.

"To meet me." He held out his hand again. "We don't have much time. Will you come with me?"

They walked together from room to room as if searching for some unknown thing. A moan sounded high on the stairway where gauzy light from a window above began to swirl. Out of the swirl appeared the filmy shape of a woman. Through undulating vapors, the apparition gazed down at them.

Ellen became aware of the tug of her companion's hand, urging her away, as if from danger. Then they were running through darkness, and she was pleading silently, *Don't let go. Don't let go of my hand....*

This time he didn't. They reached a moonlit window, and he paused and looked at her with secrets in his eyes that caused her to shiver. Behind them the window began to glow and brighten with blinding rays of light. She found herself abruptly awake in the dull safety of her room. Her limbs were dead weights, as if tired from running, and her heart felt heavier still. He was gone again. Plunged into wistful sadness, Ellen became aware of a peculiar taste in her mouth.

Her first real taste of loneliness.

2

HE FELT THE SUN warm on his shoulders, but when he reached the big old shade trees that formed a canopy over Pebble Street, the summer air felt cooler, unwelcoming. His eyes scanned the two rows of run-down houses, some boarded shut. Three children playing barefoot in the street didn't acknowledge his presence as he passed. A dog of unidentifiable heritage sauntered up, though, to sniff his leg. It responded to his touch with keen, accepting eyes and wagging tail, and fell into step at his side.

Cody Laird passed the hulls of dead cars, passed the low iron fence, rusted and leaning into a patch of flowering weeds. He stepped over potholes and crossed in front of the shell of a tiny store, its faded sign unreadable, but he knew the painted letters had once read M. G. Market. Near the far end of the street, he stopped before a narrow, two-story frame house.

He stood under the shade of a giant oak, hands in the pockets of his jeans, legs apart, eyes misting, gazing at the house. The white paint had chipped and fallen. Most of the windows were broken. It had been years since the old house had known footsteps or the sound of laughter. Once, though, four mine workers had occupied the upper bedrooms. When they worked the day shift, the men ate evening meals in the dining room with the family—a widow and her young son.

With a stab of pain, he thought of the blue flowers on the dinner plates and the aroma of baking bread, of the leathery faces of the miners and the sorrow in his mother's smile.

Cody was grateful for the dog, the only sign of friendliness. He knelt and stroked its head and neck. The shepherd's eyes and black fur edged with tan were so remarkably like old Buster's that for some moments he became lost in the deep past with his childhood companion. Warmth in his bed on winter nights, waking to a wet tongue on his face, sad canine eyes outside the school door on cold mornings, and wriggling leaps at the same door every afternoon.

"You're probably an ancestor of his," Cody said to the dog who sat at his feet. "Old Buster had his share of girlfriends in the neighborhood."

The house cast a cold shadow over them. Shivering deep within, he forced himself to look at it again. He had to see it one last time, for closure.

Why didn't the town put these dying houses out of their misery? Maybe because people still lived in some. That waitress with the pretty smile was one of them. After the remark they'd overheard at the Blue Spruce, Bill Calhoun had confirmed the girl was, indeed, a resident of Pebble Street. One wouldn't have guessed that, the way she dressed and the way she carried herself with so much pride. She had looked at him so curiously; did she recognize him? He hadn't asked her name. Maybe if he had, he would remember.

Turning his back one final time on the past, he started down the gloomy street wondering which of these pathetic old houses was hers. Through flashback habit, he had noted the identity of the truck driver who had called the woman "Pebble Princess," and had scrutinized him. He would not forget his face. Cody never forgot their faces, and, more than likely, she didn't, either. The man unknowingly had made a grave mistake, one he would likely have to answer for sometime, like so many others had; he had shot off his mouth within earshot of Cody Laird.

When the dog, who wore no collar, followed him back up the slope into the main part of town, his presence was so indelibly familiar, Cody gave it no conscious thought. His thoughts were still out recapturing the beauty of the young woman whose eyes had stolen shy and repeated glances at him last night. The stares were more than mere curiosity on her part; he detected shades of something like fear.

At the radio station on the lower end of Main Street, he was met by workmen making repairs to the interior of the building.

"The insulation is finished in the studio, Mr. Laird," one of them said.

"Good." He looked at his watch. "And just in time. I have a show to record."

"We had to order the oak lumber for the office cabinets. The company promised to deliver it from Denver day after tomorrow."

Cody nodded, making his way through the small brick building where he had ordered some minor remodeling, including removal of two interior walls, and fresh paint.

"Your dog?" a workman asked.

The animal was still at his heels. Cody looked down, smiled and shrugged. "Not that I know of."

He crossed through the refurbishing project and entered a three-room apartment at the back of the building. Renovation of these private rooms would have to wait. Meantime, he had made them reasonably comfortable with furniture he'd brought with him. There hadn't been time to concern himself with any but the basic necessities since he arrived last week, because the business itself needed more work than his living quarters. "Resurrection" was a more accurate description of what station KUBS required to get back the status of a moneymaking concern.

At the chipped kitchen sink, he rinsed the dust of Pebble Street from his hands and face, while he felt the stare of curious yellow eyes. "Well?" he asked through a towel. The dog sat down.

Cody filled a bowl with water and set it on the floor. "This is where I park myself, in case you're interested, which obviously you are. So if you have no place—you know—no place you'd rather be..." He reached out to pet the dark head. The dog licked his hand politely.

Everything was set up in the studio. He could get tonight's two-hour music program recorded before the noon news broadcast, if he didn't waste any more time. The dog had settled down on the floor after helping himself to a drink, and didn't move toward the door. Either he knew better than to follow his new pal into the studio, or he decided he had found a pleasant place to nap. Whichever it was, Cody was astonished at how the dog accepted him. It was as if he knew him. As if he had been waiting around on Pebble Street just as old Buster would have done—if he could have—to welcome his buddy home.

3

ELLEN FELT A JOLT like an electric shock when the man walked into the Blue Spruce café shortly after seven o'clock. Much of the day had been spent convincing herself he had come through town and departed, just as he had sprung unexpectedly into her dreams and gone, with an impact that penetrated her subconscious—waking or asleep—and left a mystery never to be solved.

He smiled over the heads of seated customers, smiled directly at her, as if he knew her! Well, of course, he did, if pouring coffee and setting a sandwich in front of him counted.

He slid into the same booth as before. Ellen drew a deep, shaky breath. She was both ecstatic and frightened to see him again, and self-consciously unsure of herself.

Scarcely breathing, she made herself smile and handed him a menu.

"What do you recommend?" he asked.

The voice—the same deep, resonant voice—echoed back from her dream...the most unforgettable voice she had ever heard. When he spoke, cruel warmth crept into her cheeks; she knew he could see her embarrassment and she wanted to turn and run.

"The . . . cook's special is chicken pie."

"Have you tried it?"

"Yes. It's homemade, even the crust. Really quite nice."

"Good enough." He rubbed his chin. "And plenty of bread. And black coffee."

Ellen noted the order in her head; she never used a pad and pencil. Before she responded, the deejay's voice on the radio floated out over a lull in the blended conversations of customers. She reacted with stunned disbelief and an awkward stare.

"What?" he asked.

She swallowed. This was getting too ridiculous! Her imagination had soared far out of control, so far that she actually heard herself saying, "That voice . . . on the radio . . ."

The man laughed. "You're not hearing echoes. It's my voice, recorded earlier today."

The relief brought nervous laughter. "So that's where I had heard . . . you before."

He leaned forward, and the light caught the gray of his eyes and turned them blue again. "Let me introduce myself. I'm Cody Laird."

"And you work at the radio station."

"Actually, I just bought the radio station."

"Ah. People are talking about the station having a new owner, from . . ." Her sentence ended with the unasked question.

"I moved here from Denver a week ago."

Then he lives here, he isn't just passing through. "Well, then, welcome to Shadow Valley."

Cody studied her. *She didn't remember him. Did that mean she had moved to Pebble Street in the past ten years? Hell, nobody moved to Pebble Street; people only moved away. He couldn't expect her to remember him when he'd had a different name.*

He asked, "And you are?"

Ellen nervously smoothed her white organdy apron. "Ellen Montrose."

Montrose. One of the old names on Pebble Street. He didn't remember any Ellen, but then she was several years younger and would have been just a kid when he left at the age of seventeen. Nobody remembered him—none of the respectable citizens of the town. He wanted it that way.

When she brought the coffee, he said, "Ellen Montrose, you're one of my first acquaintances in Shadow Valley. At the risk of sounding too brazen, would you consent to having dinner with me on your night off? I mean . . . you don't know me but you know who I am. Am I taking too big a risk, assuming you're not committed to some lucky guy?"

At last she was on familiar ground. Refusing dates was second nature to Ellen. "I'm afraid I have no night off," she said softly.

"What? You work every night?"

"I choose to. My school tuition is expensive." Already she had given him more information than she gave other men, but she had met him in such an unusual way. . . in such an unusual place. It wasn't easy to look into the face of someone with whom she had run breathlessly through a haunted mansion the night before—to look at him and say no.

"School?" he asked.

"Correspondence school. Fashion design. It takes . . . takes up all my spare time."

"So you can't have dinner with me."

She shook her head uneasily. "No. Sorry."

Something in her manner alerted him to the fact that more was going on here than he realized. The way she looked at him with a curiosity Cody had never seen before in a woman's eyes. The thing like fear was there, too; which made no sense because longing was also in her eyes, and she knew it and had a hard time looking directly at him. His voice lowered to a private range not much above a whisper. "Do you ever have dinner with anyone?"

"No," Ellen answered.

"For a reason?" He asked this gently, knowing her private life was none of his business and if he wasn't careful, she would tell him so. Cody had the feeling he wouldn't be the first guy she had put in his place. Yet she showed no signs of resenting him.

"I just . . . I just keep to myself is all. Busy, you know." Ellen thought, *When you've been in this town a little longer, you'll understand. We live on different sides of the tracks.* But the truth was, it didn't matter where he lived, or what he did. The man lived in Shadow Valley and she refused to risk forming any ties here. Somewhere far from this dreary place a real life awaited her.

Cody Laird was not a man to be put off easily, not when he so strongly sensed ambivalence in her mind. He was used to admiring glances from females, but this girl was different. Since he had first seen her, he had been oddly absorbed, if not mildly tormented, with the notion of getting to know her.

He waited, but only until he had finished his meal.

"I'll have more coffee, and pie," he said.

Ellen shifted with the strain of being so near him. It was awful remembering the loneliness that had fallen over her when she woke this morning and he was gone.

"What kind of pie?"

"Any kind. No, not chocolate. I hate chocolate pie."

"Cherry?"

"Naw. Too sweet."

"Banana?"

He shook his head.

"I thought you said any kind."

"Any kind except those."

"We have apple."

"No . . ."

She tried, and could not suppress a smile. "Mr. Laird, what *do* you want?"

"To have lunch with you tomorrow, since you declined dinner. Hey, a lunch is lighthearted enough, isn't it? If you'd meet me at the Silver Nugget, we could just sit at a quiet table and talk. Maybe you could tell me about your design school and I could tell you why I bought the Shadow Valley radio station. Just conversation. Okay? I'm a nice guy, Ellen. I won't lead you down any dark paths."

Won't you? You already have! The dream vibrated the very air between them—as close as the hands that had held hers in a haunted mansion. In her dream he was leading her *away* from danger. Ellen desperately wanted to know why. Her head spun with questions. If she kept her distance, there would never be answers.

"All right," she agreed. "I'll meet you for lunch tomorrow."

A massive sigh rocked his wide shoulders. "Great. Twelve o'clock?"

She nodded, feeling as giddy as a kid with a first date.

His eyes met hers in the speckled light of rustic ceiling fixtures—eyes more blue than before. A sweet, crooked smile formed on his lips. "I'll have the apple."

"What?"

"Pie."

"Oh, pie." She laughed self-consciously. "You've made a decision."

"You have, too. The right one. And I thank you."

It was his way of telling her he knew her answer hadn't been easily given. Ellen flushed. Only she could make such a big deal out of a simple lunch date. It was just that firm, locked-in agreement with herself. So many people knew about her determination to be a hermit that they didn't even bother to ask her out anymore. Only a stranger would. A stranger who couldn't know they had been together before.

Ellen began to wonder how Jeff Calhoun knew Cody Laird. Wasn't it possible that his wife might know him, too? Maybe she ought to ask Meredith. Tonight was their scheduled secret meeting—her and Meredith's. She began to hope Meredith wouldn't call it off because of some conflict with her schedule or her husband's—he often worked nights.

Meredith Calhoun phoned the café not two hours later and disguised her voice even though Ellen answered. She always changed her voice, using a different disguise each time.

"It's me. Can you come by tonight?"

"Sure." Ellen smiled. Meredith could always make her smile when she played the game of intrigue they had begun as children. They enjoyed it too much to ever reach the point of wanting to put aside the past forever.

The voice, disguised with some unidentifiable foreign accent, replied, "Good. Usual time, then. Summer place."

"Right."

"Till then." The accent had become a raspy whisper.

Ellen grinned as she put down the phone. The secrecy had begun out of necessity years ago, when she and Meredith were ten. They didn't like to admit the secrecy was still necessary, but, in actuality, it was, for the secret was their friendship.

Ellen thought back on the beginning of that friendship while she made her way across town in the darkness of a moonless night. Meredith's name had been Lockwood then; she was the only child of the bank president and the town's leading socialite. The daughter of the town's most prominent family was not allowed to have anything to do with a kid from Pebble Street.

But Meredith did find her way down to Pebble Street where the kids all had puppies and kittens. She had been enthralled by Ellen's pet mouse that rode around on her shoulder. Meredith wanted one, too—a most unthinkable thing for a Lockwood.

The family's horror at the budding friendship, and their determination to keep them apart, only encouraged the girls and elevated their friendship to a "high-secret intrigue-adventure." Their bond strengthened through the years. After Meredith returned home from finishing school, the secrecy continued because Ellen would have it no other way. Even today, the two had never been seen together in Shadow Valley.

The Lockwood family had been horrified when their daughter married a lowly veterinarian, but Ellen wasn't surprised. She knew a side to Meredith no one else knew; with her love for animals, Jeff was a perfect choice. Meredith swore that even Jeff didn't know about their friendship, but Ellen suspected he did know.

The back porch light cast a glow over the lawn—enough to see the outline of the tree house, their "summer place." The log tree-house had been there when Jeff and Meredith bought the old frame house and they had left it as it was, with the shingled roof and worn linoleum floor. In the shadows of giant trees, eerie in the moonlight, Ellen made her way up the ladder, knocking three times on the "trap door"—their time-honored signal.

Meredith knocked back and opened the rope-handled hatch. Feeling her way, Ellen climbed in, and as soon as the hatch was closed, Meredith turned on her flashlight. A tiny woman with short auburn hair and green eyes, she gave her friend a quick hug and motioned for Ellen to sit down on one of the two pillows she had brought up earlier. They sat close together in the small space, facing each other.

"I've missed you," Meredith said, handing Ellen a cola.

"I've missed you, too." She snapped open the can. "What have you been up to all summer?"

"Helping Jeff. He's trying to open a new office in Boville and train a technician to run it, so he won't have to go over there so much except for emergencies. I've been scouting for office space—that sort of thing." She set down her can of cola and reached for Ellen's hand, squeezing hard. "What's happening with you? Aren't you about finished with your design course?"

"Just about. That and work are my life." Ellen rested her back on the rough wall of the tree house. "Well, almost. I had a strange experience. I don't know what it means, but I have to tell someone and you're the only one I can tell. Besides, there's a chance you might know him."

"Him?" Meredith straightened. "Him who?"

"A guy who bought the radio station. He was in the café with Jeff. They seemed to be friends. Do you know him?"

"No . . . although Jeff and I have talked about the radio station being under new ownership and the changes going on there. Jeff said he knew the owner, but Jeff knows everybody five minutes after they arrive in town."

"I wonder why," Ellen said.

"Why what?"

"Why Jeff knows him. Maybe he has a pet. A dog. He's more the dog type than the cat type, I think—"

Meredith interrupted with a hand on her shoulder. "Ellen, what are you going on about this guy for? What happened?"

"He asked me out and cajoled me into saying yes."

"Well! That beats all! I thought you had a rule. A stupid rule, but a rule nonetheless. I've never heard you talk about a guy before, either, since about tenth grade. What gives?"

"I don't know if you'll believe it. I hardly do myself. The truth is, I had a dream about this guy the night *before* he came into the café. Isn't that weird? And then after I saw him, I dreamed about him again, and back he came again yesterday."

Meredith was hugging her knees. She said in a flat tone of disbelief, "You dreamed about a guy before you met him."

"Crazy but true. We were in the Whitfield mansion, and the ghost was there. I seemed to belong there. We both belonged there, and yet we didn't. I couldn't believe it when the very same guy walked into the café!"

"Wait, wait, wait! You dreamed about the mansion? A guy in the mansion! Omigod! It's like the prediction of long ago!"

Ellen's stomach went weak. "What prediction?"

"Mine! My prediction about you and the mansion. Remember? You were so obsessed with the place and I had my new Tarot deck that predicted you would be queen of that mansion and there would be a handsome king."

"Good grief, Mere. We were making it up. You didn't even know how to use the cards yet."

"I wasn't making it up. I was following the instruction book. It was *there*."

"We were children then. They were all childhood fantasies."

Meredith seemed quite unnerved. "But you had the dream. And then the guy . . . who walked in and asked you to dinner, even though he didn't know you. Or did he? Know you?"

"No, of course not. He's a stranger in Shadow Valley."

Silence filled the dark tree house. At last Meredith drew in her breath. "It's a sign! Some kind of sign. Or maybe a warning. Tell me about the dream. Was it scary . . . with the ghost? Details. I want details!"

Meredith knew about warning signs. Ellen rationalized Meredith's second sight by calling it superstition, and it was superstition, to be sure. But it was more. Meredith had hung around the gypsy woman when she was a kid, always fascinated by the gypsy's strange powers. Meredith herself was soon trying to communicate with spirits of the dead and tell fortunes by cards and tea leaves. She was the only person with whom Ellen shared her sighting of the ghost of Whitfield mansion, because as a child she'd considered Mere an expert on such things.

"The details?" Meredith demanded again.

Ellen had relived the dream a hundred times. "The mansion wasn't run-down. It was gilded and magnificent. He appeared on the stairway and held out his hand to me but I was afraid because the ghost was in the house. I drew back because of the awful sounds in the house, and he disappeared when I resisted."

Meredith processed this information like a scientist gathering data in a lab. "Hmm. And the second dream?"

"In the second—after I had met him—dust and cobwebs filled the mansion, as if no one had been there for a long time. He was inside and called out my name. He said he had been waiting for me and wanted me to come with him—again. We walked around inside and the ghost was following us and we ran...and I woke up."

"This is no coincidence, Ellen. It can't be. Something about that mansion has always haunted you."

"*He* haunts me, too—just his voice on the radio."

"You mean the new *voice*? No guy could look like that one sounds. Even in a dream."

"He could, believe me."

"Omigod! And you've broken your resolve—your blood oath—not to date anybody in Shadow Valley. We have to get to the bottom of this dream phenomenon."

"I've never met anyone like him," Ellen admitted. "He makes me feel all these strange...things...."

Meredith opened a second cola. "I don't know about this, Ellen. You're starting to sound human. The first thing you know, you're going to be discovering all kinds of things you've denied yourself."

A picture formed in Ellen's mind of herself and Cody Laird sitting across the table from each other. She savored the image more than she wished to. "There isn't time for discovering anything, even if I wanted to. I'm working on my last assignment, then I'll get my diploma."

"Something strange is going on here," Meredith said. "A stranger in your old mansion beckoning you from the dreamscape . . . and the mansion covered in cobwebs is symbolic of your not having thought about it for a long time."

"One grows up," Ellen said.

"Not always. Our friendship is the same secret liaison as before. Dreams don't have to grow up, do they?"

Ellen nodded, trying to remember the exact point in her life when she stopped going to the mansion—it wasn't long after she and Meredith had stopped going there together.

"I'm going to ask Jeff about the new owner of the radio station and see what I can find out about him. This is all very eerie. How can you be so calm about it?"

"I'm not calm. I'm trying to act calm. I wanted to just run from it, Mere, not get to know this guy because it scares me. But he wouldn't let me get away with that. I found I couldn't say no to him."

Lights shone in the driveway, announcing Jeff's arrival. "Yikes, he's early," Meredith said. "I'd better get myself down out of this tree house." She took her friend's hand. "Something is going to happen at that lunch. I can feel it."

This frightened Ellen, because Meredith was never wrong about her psychic impressions. She asked, "Is it good or bad?"

"I can't tell. I can just feel an intensity. A tremendous intensity. Something strange."

"Fine. Thanks a lot." Ellen was on the ladder. Now that her eyes were used to the darkness, she didn't need a flashlight. The moonlight was enough.

"You've got to let me know what happens at lunch," Meredith said, following right behind her.

4

WHAT TO WEAR WASN'T a problem, except for deciding. She stood in the open doorway of her closet, eyeing the choices.

What to wear. The Silver Nugget, located on the lower floor of the hotel, was the only truly nice restaurant in Shadow Valley. Ellen had never set foot in the place. During the three years of her design course, she had completed several dozen outfits of all styles and fabrics and never worn any of them. They were the clothes of her portfolio. Saved for New York.

This might be interesting, after all, she thought. A chance to wear one of her high-fashion designs. A chance to eat in a place where manners would count. After all those memorized books on etiquette, it would be refreshing to jump the gun on New York, and step out of the drab and faceless role she was born into. With far and away the best-looking guy in the whole town! Plenty of eyes would be on them. Eyes of the social register, ogling.

She took out a white linen summer suit and a paisley silk scarf cut from a dress imported from Paris decades ago. Owners of thrift shops usually didn't recognize superexpensive fabric in outdated clothes.

People rarely looked beyond the obvious. Her room, for instance, would have been a surprise to anyone viewing the dilapidated house from outside. Flower-patterned wallpaper in tones of pink and mint green covered the wall cracks. The old furniture and a glass-front cabinet were painted white. Lace curtains, purchased from Goodwill and hand-washed monthly, hung at the windows, and leafy potted plants were placed where the morning sun could touch them. On a table fashioned from an old door was her grandmother's sewing machine. Clothing patterns and a few fashion magazines were stacked neatly on a shelf. Three unmatched throw rugs covered the worn wood floor.

She glanced in the mirror, wondering whether or not to change her hair. "Eyelash curler," she reminded her reflection. For months it had been on her "should have" list. Today was the occasion to splurge.

She found her grandfather pulling weeds from his flower beds in the front yard. Theirs was the only tended yard within view; Emory Montrose had a special knack for gardening. In summer he picked his own fresh flowers for their breakfast table. "I have a short errand in town, Gramps. Anything you need?"

"Tobacco," the old man replied without looking up.

It was an eight-minute walk into town. This morning the sun was shining in a cloudless sky. Normally, she would be bent over the sewing machine or studying her books, but it was not like other mornings. Her mind was adrift in memories from a dream—air-drawn mirages. Even Meredith's impressions and warnings weren't going to get her down.

Mr. Post, owner of the drugstore, always had a smile for her. "Morning, Ellen. Fine day."

"Good morning."

He said, "The new *Vogue* is here. I've promised the copies to Mrs. Stewardham, but if you want to look it over, she'll never know the difference."

"Thanks, I will." The magazine was probably not promised at all, but Mr. Post knew she couldn't afford to buy it. He had been allowing her to look through the magazines for years and never mentioned to anyone that he did so.

A belted jersey dress caught her eye. On her sketch pad, she quickly, expertly, copied the design to study later, grateful no other customers were in the store. Setting the magazine back with care, she purchased an eyelash curler—the first she had ever owned—and her grandfather's favorite brand of tobacco.

Back in the privacy of her room, she tried the curler, blinking, pleased at the results. She pulled her blond hair away from her face and put on her grandmother's antique pearl earrings, and took longer than usual with her nails.

She held out her hands and blew on the light pink polish, wondering what it could be about an old mining town hunkered between mountain peaks that attracted a man like Cody Laird.

"Or for that matter," she asked her reflection, "what about *me* attracts him?"

SHE ENTERED THE HOTEL at exactly twelve o'clock, thinking he would already be seated in the restaurant. Instead, he was waiting for her in the plush lobby and was on his feet the moment she passed through the carved double doors. He came toward her wearing dark slacks and a sports jacket and a smile. And a tie. A date with a man wearing a tie? It was a day of firsts.

Cody, ill-prepared for discovering such high style after the little white apron and the Pebble Princess label, was thunderstruck.

"You look stunning," he said softly, reaching for her hand.

Exactly as he had done in her dream. And she accepted it with some hesitation, just like before.

"Our table is ready."

The windows of the Silver Nugget Hotel restaurant were located just under the ceiling, so the lighting was soft. Candles flickered on the tables. The chandeliers were not lighted.

Cody held the chair for her, like men did in the movies. It was fantasy enough the way he had appeared in her life, but all this . . .

He even asked if she had a preference of wine, and when she shook her head dazedly, he ordered a bottle by name, and tasted it before the waiter filled her glass with pale gold bubbles.

He raised his goblet and said simply, "Cheers."

"Cheers." Ellen began to relax. It seemed so natural being in this unfamiliar setting, and natural being here with him. She felt more at ease in the Silver Nugget Hotel than she ever had in the truck stop. No cooking smells or gruff voices or truck engines starting. No radio music here; no music at all.

They ordered Caesar salads and shrimp prepared in wine sauce, after which Cody gulped his wine and sat back to study the beautiful woman seated across from him. Her blue eyes were sparkling in the candle flickers. All those years in Denver, he had never met anyone who affected him like this woman did. Who would ever have thought in Shadow Valley . . .

"Tell me about your school, then," he coaxed.

"I'm studying to be a fashion designer. By correspondence. I'm finishing my eighth and last class, actually, which consists mainly of preparing my portfolio. You know, a collection of my designs. The suit I'm wearing is one of them."

Cody sat forward. "You're kidding! You designed this? Who made it?"

"I did, of course. I've been making my clothes since I was twelve."

"I'll be damned. This is real talent, Ellen."

"Thanks." She grinned, flattered.

"A hotshot fashion designer right here in Shadow Valley."

She laughed. "That's almost a contradiction in terms. I won't be staying here. The jobs are in New York and Paris.

I'll start with New York." When he looked at her curiously, she added, "Don't laugh. I have big dreams."

This was not good news for him, although he had wondered since yesterday what a girl like Ellen Montrose was doing with losers who still occupied the old mine-workers' houses.

"What's keeping you in Shadow Valley, then?" he asked.

"My grandfather. I'm the only one he has. He and my grandmother raised me after my father was killed in the mine and my mother had a breakdown and left. So I'll be here for him for as long as he lives." She took several sips from her glass. "Which might not be very long. He's not well at all. Sometimes I see him staring up at the mountains with such a faraway look in his eyes and I know he's thinking of my grandmother and my father and missing them terribly. It's hard to get old."

Cody nodded. "How does your grandfather feel about your big plans?"

"He approves totally. I won't allow him to feel guilty for holding me here, though. I tell him I'm not ready, that I have to complete my studies. He doesn't know I'll be finished in only a few weeks." She took another swallow, amazed at how good the wine tasted, and how it relaxed her.

He refilled her empty glass, and his own.

She said, "Why are we talking only about me? As I recall, you promised to tell me why you bought the radio station."

"It was bankrupt. Gone under. And there didn't seem to be any other interested buyers. Which, boiled down, meant I could afford it. I had worked for a station in Denver, worked my way up to manager, so I learned every aspect of the business. I've got ideas for this little old station that will put Shadow Valley on the map. I mean to pump some life into this place. Of course, first I have to wake it up before I can do any jump-starting."

"The new programming."

"It's barely started. I need a little time to win over the city fathers. I thought they might fight me a little, but so far, they're with me. A town like this needs positive input to keep it going."

She touched the scarf at her neck, luxuriating in the feel of the silk, and asked, "But why Shadow Valley? When there are so many other towns you could have gone to."

"You don't like this town."

"No."

He shrugged, but the shrug was an act because he understood perfectly why she would hate it. He had felt the same, once. It wasn't a subject she would want to discuss, and neither did he. "The town does have possibilities. And, like I said, I could afford the station. The last manager rode the business into the ground. He didn't know the ropes of broadcasting. I do."

"He didn't have a voice like yours, either," she said with a chuckle, her head so light with wine, it had lost much of the faculty of censorship.

"That sounds like a compliment, pretty lady."

"No question about it. You don't sound like Shadow Valley. I'd never have imagined it was a local voice. But then, technically, it isn't."

Was this the opening he had been looking for? He wanted to tell her that his voice—along with the rest of him—was, technically, local. But she was so relaxed with the wine and obviously enjoying herself. It wasn't the time to bring up the subject of Pebble Street; not here. Ellen had, for the hour at least, escaped, and he had no right to send her emotions reeling back there.

So, instead, he ordered another bottle of wine.

"Really, I shouldn't," she protested mildly, but by this time the main course had come, and they decided wine was needed to enjoy it properly.

She asked him about Denver.

"I started out as a guitarist in a small band," Cody said. "We played minor clubs here and there, and I began working as a deejay for parties and clubs. I was nineteen when I was hired by a radio station to do an early-morning show with another guy, and when the band moved on, I stayed and made it a point to learn everything I could about the business. In six years I was assistant manager."

"How old are you now?"

"Twenty-eight."

"You could pass for over thirty."

He grinned. "I have done, often enough."

She grinned back at him. "And I could pass for twenty-one."

This remark took away his breath as if he'd been punched. "Good God, don't tell me you're not twenty-one!"

"I'm not twenty-one. I'm twenty-four."

"Damn it, don't scare me like that."

"What's so scary about it?"

Cody laughed. "Never mind."

She pushed her plate aside although not much was eaten, and leaned forward, fingering the base of her wine goblet. "I have a confession to make, Mr. Cody Laird...." Hesitating thoughtfully, she twisted the goblet faster. "I've never known anybody named Cody before, except Buffalo Bill, and that doesn't count because it was his surname. And it wouldn't count anyway, because I didn't know Buffalo Bill Cody personally."

He was watching the light dancing in her eyes and the way her lips moved when she spoke. "Is that your confession? That you don't know anybody else named Cody?"

"No! Of course not." She sipped from the glass and set it down. "My confession is that I had a dream about you. I wasn't going to tell you, but the wine impedes my . . . my restraint."

He made himself resist the urge to reach for her hands across the table, although it was becoming more difficult by the minute not to touch her. Cody had begun imagining how her eyes would look in ripples of sunlight or drenched with morning dew. Or how her hair would feel between his fingers. Or how her lips would taste. He asked, "Why didn't you want to tell me?"

"About my dream? Well, because it was very odd."

This time she wasn't teasing. The mention of the dream brought to her eyes that same expression of confusion he had seen in the Blue Spruce. "Tell me the dream," he said gently.

Ellen stared at him for an uncomfortable time, as if she were wrestling with control and censoring her response. Finally, she began, "You must have seen the mansion on the hill north of town. . . ."

"The Whitfield mansion. Sure. It was built by the first owner of the Shadow Valley mine."

"It's empty. For sale."

"I saw the sign. Why?"

"I dreamed about the mansion. You were in it."

"In the mansion?"

"Uh-huh. It was you, all right."

"What was I doing there?"

"I have no idea."

He could no longer control the urge, and reached across the table to close his hand over hers. The second he touched her, he witnessed a change in Ellen. She twitched involuntarily; her hand quivered. His natural response was to press harder, protectively, reassuringly, and when he did, she calmed. What had frightened her, though, when he first touched her?

He asked, "Were you there? At the mansion?"

She shook herself back to the glossy reality of the moment, trying to ignore the fact that his touch felt exactly in real life as it had in her dream. "We both were there," she said dazedly. "And someone else. A ghost, I think."

Fascinated and flattered, Cody decided he must have made more of an impression on her that first night he happened into the café than he realized. He smiled to put her at ease. "What happened?"

Ellen was gazing abstractedly at his hand clasped over hers. "Nothing," she replied without moving, wondering if he could detect the lie. "You disappeared and then I woke up."

"Umm. Why the mansion, do you think? Were you ever in it?"

"No, but as a child I often imagined what it would be like inside. I used to tell myself I'd live in a mansion someday."

"Maybe you will." He felt warmth pulsing into her hands, where moments before they had been cool. "If that's what you want."

"It is. What's the point of dreaming small when the world is so big?"

"I know about dreams, myself," he volunteered.

She leaned closer. "Real dreams or sleep dreams?"

Her nearness was causing uncomfortable tugs through his body. The closeness was making him crazy. But he wasn't ready yet to release her hand because a disturbing and relentless voice somewhere in his head was warning him not to let go. The voice was like a wisp of memory reminding him that if he released her hand, she would disappear—maybe forever.

"I don't dream in my sleep, Ellen. I wish I did, because I'd like nothing better than to fall asleep and dream about you."

She blushed. "Everyone dreams."

"I don't."

"Of course, you do. Maybe you just don't recall your dreams."

Cody shook his head, deep in thought. "I used to dream when I was a kid. I had a recurring nightmare that scared me green, so my mother taught me how to forget my dreams and I haven't remembered any since."

"Really? What was the nightmare?"

He looked at her blankly. "I forgot it."

"Well, there, you see. It's not that you don't dream, you just are unaware."

"Same thing, as far as I'm concerned."

Draining her glass, Ellen said, "My dreams have a very weird quality. Time-wise."

"What does that mean?"

"I can't explain it. And I'd better not try. My tongue is somewhat out of control, thanks to this lovely tasting wine."

"Would you like coffee?"

Ellen looked about the room, aware that people were watching them, whispering about them. Nothing went unnoticed in Shadow Valley and no one would be watched more fervently than the town's handsome new bachelor. The eligible ladies of repute, of which the mayor's daughter was one, were bound to see to it that Mr. Laird was soon—tomorrow-soon—informed as to the quality of the company he was keeping. So she'd better enjoy this lunch. What brand of social quality did the guy expect, though, when he befriended a waitress at a truck stop?

None of it mattered, anyway. A lunch was all she had promised. "If you don't mind, I think fresh air would do me more good than coffee right now."

This suggestion pleased him. He signaled for the waiter. "Let's take a walk, then. The weather's perfect."

When he reluctantly lifted his hand from hers, Ellen experienced the same dismal sensation of emptiness that had harrowed her after last night's dream. The sudden sensation of loneliness was a wallop to everything she had ever known as security. It was too intense for understanding, too painful for her well-being. This guy wasn't good for her! He brought only confusion to her life. Her own emotions, for God's sake, had gone spiraling way out of control.

Her attractive, distractive companion left some bills on the small tray, rose, and came around the table, where he offered her his arm.

He's not sure how steady I'll be on my feet, Ellen thought with a private giggle. *Bless his sweet, attentive heart.* In actuality, her composure was steadfast, dignity unwavering. Touching him, like before, gave her an anchor and buoyancy at the same time.

At the bottom of the hotel steps Cody was met by a wriggling canine, who commanded an elaborate greeting and got it.

Ellen joined Cody in the exuberant welcome. "Your dog, obviously."

"Just a friend."

The yellow eyes were appraising her brazenly. She asked, "What's his name?"

"I call him Buster."

"Hmm. I knew a Buster when I was a kid. He looked rather similar to this guy."

Sure, she would have known him, Cody thought. *Old Buster was friendly with all the kids.* So Ellen remembered his dog and not him. And he didn't remember her. It was the age difference, of course; five years between kids was a profound gap. An older one was too occupied with being the tough guy to acknowledge the bothersome younger children.

Under the cloudless blue sky, Buster jogged along beside them, down the sidewalk, to the park in the town center. An aroma of late-blooming lilacs mingled with fresh mountain pine. The grass was soft and springy under their feet. They walked past the swings and slide to the shady slope above the round white bandstand.

She asked, "Does your friend live with you?"

"He seems to think so. From the way he latched on to me, I can only assume he doesn't belong to anybody."

She mused, "Dogs know."

"Know what?"

"About people. Their instincts serve them much better than ours do. If we even have any." She leaned against the trunk of a quaking aspen and gazed up at the play of spangled sunlight through the leaves. "My head feels clearer. I don't know why I drank so much wine."

"Hell, because you just wanted to. What's wrong with that?"

"It makes me giddy. I hate feeling out of control. Do you feel it, too?"

"Sure," he lied. He had been feeling out of control, all right, but not from the wine. He was used to wine, but not to what had been going on in his head and his body for the past hour.

She asked, "Don't you have to go to work?"

"Pretty soon. What about you?"

"My shift starts at two."

He looked at his watch. One-twenty. "Can I walk you home?" He asked knowing she would decline.

"No," she answered quickly. "Don't bother. I . . . want to make a couple of stops on the way, and I'm sure you're facing a busy afternoon."

"When can we do this again?"

Ellen's heart sank. She forced herself to look at him. "The bargain was for one lunch, Cody."

"This was just for openers, wasn't it?"

"I can't..." Her gaze lowered to the ground. "I can't see you again."

"Will you explain that?" He frowned. "I haven't seen any signs of revulsion on your part. In fact, it's the opposite."

Tears formed in her eyes the instant she looked back at him. "It's not you, it's me. It's because I'm going to leave—"

"You haven't left yet."

Her words were so weighted with sadness, she could scarcely get them out. Probably they wouldn't make sense to anyone but her. But he deserved honesty; or at least, as much honesty as she dared. It was impossible to tell him how terrified she was of her own emotions. Every movement of his body, every syllable from his mouth assailed her senses with forbidden promises. His deep, velvet voice was a lullaby wrapping her in unspoken caresses. His hypnotic eyes absorbed the colors of hers, mysteriously taking possession of them. And what was his heart doing? Wilfully timing its beats in synchronization with her own? *Or was it the other way around?*

"How can I explain?" she murmured. "My life has only one purpose—to find my way to a better place. I have no ties here, other than my grandfather, so when he's gone I will turn my back on Shadow Valley and never look back. I'm frightened of anything that threatens to make leaving more difficult."

His words came gently. "You're frightened of having a friend?"

"Not a friend. You."

He knew exactly what she meant; there was nothing to gain by pretending otherwise. Ellen admitted to keeping clear of any matters of the heart; she didn't understand what was happening to her and couldn't deal with it—didn't want to. He said, "So nothing can interfere with your plans."

"Nothing. Cody, here my life is . . . is wrong. I don't belong here. I've never belonged here." She wiped at a tear on her cheek. Why did the plea for freedom hurt so much? "Oh, I couldn't expect anyone to really understand. . . ."

But he did understand. He knew the sound of taunts and ridicule, the echoes of those hateful names. *White trash.* Even now, the words hurt, and filled him with rage. People he saw now on the streets—people he went to school with—didn't recognize him because the kids of Pebble Street had no proper names and no faces. He was out of the role now. He was somebody with an investment the town needed and welcomed. The stigma of their birthplace would have taken an even heavier toll on a girl who couldn't use her fists to retaliate. Cody felt her pain all the way into his soul. Oh, yes, he understood.

He knew the need for freedom from pain. Ellen had to find the freedom to be who she was born to be. She wouldn't agree to a relationship with him because she couldn't bear to be distracted from the dreams she lived for. Damn it to hell, he did understand. And he'd try to hold her anyway. He'd hold her any way he could.

"I wouldn't try to hold you here," he said, realizing she knew it was a lie.

"I'm sorry," Ellen said haltingly. "The part of me that isn't scared is really sorry. I like you, Cody. . . ."

"You like me too much."

"Yes . . ."

"And that's why we can't get together again."

"Yes."

"Firm?"

She nodded. "Please don't make it any more difficult than it is."

He scowled from frustration, not anger. "If that's how you want it." *He would think of some way to persuade her; he had* to. *Since the moment she walked into the hotel today, looking like she belonged anywhere but Shadow Valley, he had known he didn't want to live his life without her.*

She bent down to the dog, who had not left Cody's side. "Goodbye, Buster. You'll take good care of my friend, won't you?"

From the edge of the park, Ellen turned around. The man and the dog had not moved from their spot on the slope. She raised her hand in a wave, grateful that Cody was too far away to see the tears streaming down her cheeks.

Curse it! The voice in Cody's head was so deafening it hurt through his whole body. *Damn it! Why did I let go of her hand?*

THAT NIGHT HE CAME to her again.

Dressed in a tuxedo, he was smiling up at her from the elegant foyer of the Whitfield mansion, as she descended the curving stairway. She was wearing a white gown, and jewels in her hair. Her footsteps made no sound on the carpeted stairs. When she saw him, her heart began to beat fast, and her steps quickened.

"Ellen," he said. "Our table is ready."

The touch of his hand was warm and protective as she was led into a dining room swimming in crystal prisms. A massive arrangement of lilacs and pine branches adorned a table set with sparkling china and crystal and magnificent silver. There were two chairs only, but place settings for three. Three? Confused, Ellen gazed around the room until her eyes fixed on a shadow moving along a far wall. It formed the hint of a human form as it drifted, and a chill wafted in its wake. That thing again! That ghost . . . following them. Why? Was it evil? Did it want them out of here? Why a third setting with no chair at the table?

They did not sit down. As the eerie chill coiled through the room, Cody led her nearer the stone hearth where a fire blazed with welcoming warmth. He proceeded to pour champagne into long-stemmed goblets. His voice echoed as if from stereo speakers when he spoke, handing her a goblet. "I will never quench my thirst, Ellen. And neither will you. Champagne, like life, is filled with bubbles that burst when they touch the lips—there are always more . . . and there will never be enough. . . ."

When she had sipped, with the bubbles tickling her throat, he took the drink from her and set both goblets on the mantel. Shadows of the fireplace flames moved across his face, and in the pale light his eyes were starry blue. The gnawing desires within her rose and filled her heart as she felt herself being pulled into his arms—strong, sheltering arms. . . .

His heart was beating in time with hers and his lips moved over hers and all the crystal prisms fell over them and danced around their heads, and she drew in the taste of his power and his magic and heard her own voice whispering, "Please, don't go. . . ."

PRISMS OF LACE-FILTERED sunlight twinkled over her face and the pink-and-white bedspread. Her thin curtain moved in the early-morning breeze, causing prisms to dance. As the sun forced the day upon her, Ellen sat up groggily. The room blurred through light and tears.

My freedom has a higher price than I could ever have imagined, she sobbed into the memory of her dream. *It hurts. It hurts so badly. . . .*

5

IN SPITE OF ALL HER trying and great efforts at denying, the
hurt stuck stubbornly to her throughout the morning. It ad-
hered to every stitch of thread and caused her to forget what
she was sewing. Why would she have a dream about leaving
a man she barely knew? And why would the dream fill her
with such emptiness?

How could things have changed so fast?

Morning sunlight, golden beams,
Show me riches, show me dreams.
Sunlight, shine a path for me
Toward the place I'm meant to be....

"Something is bothering you today," Emory Montrose said,
as he watched Ellen rinse their breakfast plates under the tap.

"I'm just distracted, Gramps. Concentrating on my sewing."

"You will be getting your certification soon."

Pain wedged in her throat. He had always sensed her rest-
lessness and it worried him to think of her having to stay on
for his sake, when she didn't want to be here. Ellen never
spoke of leaving to her grandfather. But he knew.

"I have an awful lot to do yet," she lied. "Some special assignments and an exam." And she changed the subject. "You
slept late today, Gramps. Are you feeling okay?"

"It's the cool mornings." The old man lit his pipe and sat
back in front of the window, gazing out at the high moun-

tain peaks. The look in his eyes was one Ellen recognized; he was remembering long-ago days when all of the family was here and the silver mine was in operation. He said, "I can feel winter coming on. My toes are getting stiff."

"It's barely July," she said gently. "But this morning was pretty cool." Actually, it was a warm morning for the heights of Colorado. Gramps didn't feel the warmth as he always had before. "I'll get out another quilt for you before I go to work this afternoon." Ellen quickly dried the plates and set the skillet upside down on the cracked tile countertop to dry.

She turned and watched the old man stroke his beard as he puffed. "Are you going outside to the garden?" she asked. "The sun is shining."

"It won't be for long. It'll cloud up. There's a storm heading in."

She glanced through the windowpanes at the bright sky above the mountains. Not all of Gramps' predicted storms actually happened. Her grandmother had died during a summer storm, and sometimes these past months, Gramps saw darkness above him where there was none. Sometimes he shivered in sunlight.

"I'm going to mend the hinge on the back door today," the old man said. "Gotta keep the place up."

For what? she thought. *It's destined to become a corpse like all the others....* Once again, Ellen was reminded from where she'd acquired her unrelenting pride. His was now delusional.

Was hers, too?

Were the aspirations of a glorious career and recognition for her talents no more than desperate fantasies? No! Hadn't the school instructors nominated her outstanding designs for an award? They had, and she was going to win it, too! Damn these spooky night dreams for kicking up doubts. She'd never had doubts before.

"Kill doubts!" she muttered, climbing the stairs to her room and her sketches and her award-waiting clothes and her portfolio and her hopes for escape into the world of Success.

ON HER WAY TO WORK, Ellen was waylayed at the edge of the park by a mysterious figure wearing a yellow hooded slicker motioning to her from behind a line of high hedges.

"Ellen! Over here!" the breathy voice called.

She was used to Meredith's drama antics, although this "disguise" on a day darkening with rain clouds was hardly outrageous. Meredith just liked the game, always had, since she first realized her association with Ellen was forbidden. High adventure in those days, now it amounted to little more than a private joke and a reminder of Meredith's attempts at eccentricity.

Smiling, Ellen ducked behind the trees, to be met by Meredith's complaints. "You didn't call! I had to come after you in broad daylight to find out what happened on your lunch date yesterday. How could you leave me dangling in suspense like that?"

"I did try calling once. You weren't home and I wasn't about to leave a message."

Meredith was squeezing her arm. "So? Tell me!"

Ellen grinned. "I had too much wine to drink and made a fool of myself."

"You? Drinking in public? What kind of influence does this guy have? Did you get tipsy enough to confess to him about the dreams?"

"Actually, yes. I told him I dreamed about him and the mansion, only I left out the part about the dream before I met him. I didn't think he'd believe it and if he did, he might have made too much of it."

"Too much of it? Really? Of something that can't happen?"

Ellen felt the awful sting of unhappiness that had never been part of her life before—a feeling of something being terribly wrong. "It was bad enough as it was, Mere. He wants to see me again. And I want to see him. And I can't. I don't dare. I just don't need the . . . confusion."

"Something happened, didn't it?"

"I don't know what happened. I look into his eyes and I don't know what to think. I don't dare think. There's something about him that bothers me—a man who doesn't dream himself but shows up in mine. I'm uncomfortable with it."

"I would be, too," Meredith said. "What do you mean, he doesn't dream?"

"He says he doesn't."

"How can that be true? Maybe he's some kind of warlock putting a spell on you. Warlocks don't dream; they control other people's dreams by getting inside them. Did you mention the ghost?"

"Yes. He barely blinked, as if that was nothing." She frowned at the suggestion Cody might be a warlock. Why did Meredith always have to get so carried away with the bizarre? Even so . . . in spite of that, her input on unexplainable matters was welcome, even sought. Ellen continued, "Last night I dreamed again of us in the mansion and the table was set for three instead of two, and the ghost was there, following us, as if it were her house and we were dinner guests, but we didn't feel welcome."

"I think the ghost is luring you to the mansion. Maybe it has something to do with the fact that you don't go around there much anymore. She's trying to entice you back and using this guy to do it," Meredith said.

"But that's crazy. The ghost never knew me."

"She must have. Otherwise she wouldn't be invading your dreams."

Ellen stared at Meredith's face behind the slicker hood. "It's creepy and I don't like it. But I like Cody. He's fascinating and sophisticated and worldly. Nothing like Shadow Valley men."

Pushing a strand of hair from her eyes, Meredith said, "If you want my opinion, the Whitfield ghost knows him, too. I wonder if he knows anything about the mansion."

"How could he? He's new here."

"Just the same . . . there has to be some connection somewhere. Is the guy interested in you? He is, isn't he, Ellen?"

She flushed, unwittingly flattered beyond measure. "He is—more than makes sense. He was not a bit happy when I told him I was leaving. Did you ask Jeff what he knew about him?"

"I brought up the subject of the new radio-station owner but Jeff had nothing to volunteer except that the guy has big ideas about changes. I don't think he knows anything about his personal life, or at least he wasn't saying anything, and you know how Jeff loves to talk." Meredith shifted her eyes to see if anyone was lurking in the park, watching them. "Something is mighty damn strange. When are you going to see him again?"

"I'm not. I can't. I just can't. It could threaten my sanity. I'm going to forget about him."

At that moment Ellen heard a yelp and felt something brush against her leg. Startled, she looked down. "Buster! What are you doing here?" She whirled around in time to meet the penetrating blue eyes of Cody Laird.

He was already upon them, having approached from the far end of the park, just across from the radio station. It was too late for Meredith to duck away. The young man looked at her quizzically before he turned his gaze back to Ellen.

"Hi," he said.

Did he know she would be passing through here on her way to work, or was he just out walking with old Buster after lunch? Chances were, it was the former. Ellen's heart began thudding just at the sight of him. No man had a right to do this to her; to make her feel so giddy and unsure of herself....

"Hello," she replied.

He glanced again at the figure in yellow plastic, a tiny, red-haired woman who was staring at him with such intensity he felt uneasy. "I haven't had the pleasure," he said.

So they had been discovered in one of their rare public meetings. "Uh...Cody Laird, this is Meredith..." Ellen said haltingly.

"Calhoun," Meredith said, extending her hand. The slicker crackled with the movement. "I'm glad to meet the new voice of Shadow Valley in person." Her eyes scanned the sky. "Looks like a storm coming," she said. "I never take chances. I'm deathly allergic to rain. Have to keep dry."

"That ensemble should do it." He smiled. "Calhoun. Any relation to Jeff?"

"Spouse of Jeff. Part-time veterinary assistant. Sometime accountant."

Self-styled sometime psychic and reader of fortunes, Ellen wanted to add, and might have, had she not been remembering the huddle Cody and Jeff were in at the café booth, discussing what seemed to be important business. He no doubt was already thinking that Dr. Calhoun's wife was a bit eccentric. Which wouldn't bother Meredith in the least; she considered her "studied eccentricity" a trademark.

"Well," Meredith said, studying the man intensely, without shame. "Ellen Montrose and I were just casually passing by each other and stopped to comment on the sky. I'll be on my way." She turned, then turned back. "Hey. Play 'Rainy Day People' for me next program, will you, Cody? That song always puts me in a sunny mood." She pulled the hood down over her eyes as if it were raining.

"Sure thing." He smiled again.

They watched the shiny yellow figure disappear, not down the sidewalk, but through the trees in the park.

"I never heard of anyone being allergic to rain," Cody mused. "Especially when it isn't raining."

Ellen shrugged. More than once she had suggested to Meredith that the game of so many years ought to stop, but Meredith liked the fun. There wasn't enough to laugh about in Shadow Valley, she always said. After today, being caught like this, Ellen would again suggest putting an end to the spy game, but such an incident would only spur Meredith on. Getting "caught" was probably the greatest fun of all.

"On your way to work?" Cody asked.

She nodded.

"We'll walk with you, Buster and I."

He fell into step beside her while the dog ran ahead, sniffing at shrubs along the way. "I've been thinking about you a lot since yesterday," he said.

"Thinking what?" *Should I have asked that?* the voice inside her head screamed as soon as the words were out. The truth was, every syllable from her mouth sounded like a musical discord, a wrong note. She who had prided herself on her self-assured image didn't know what to say to Cody Laird. She feared her own voice and what he read or didn't read into each fumbled word. *What was happening to her?*

"Thinking how beautiful you are," he replied. "Thinking how much I liked being with you and wishing I could see you every day. Knowing it frustrates you when I say that. Ellen, what you say to me and what I see in your eyes don't match—it's like hearing the wrong words to the right music."

Wrong notes. How did he know she was thinking about wrong notes? Were their minds that much alike? Or could he read her mind? Her head was all but spinning. She wanted to tell him about their tryst last night in her sleep and the lurking ghost and the table set for three. She wanted to ask him what he thought about it. But of course, she couldn't. What point was there in her relating her dreams of him and encouraging him all the more?

"You're a persistent guy," she said.

"I didn't get where I am in this world by being meek. A man has to know what he wants."

"And you're used to getting what you want."

"I've learned to get what I want, yeah."

"So have I," she said. "Or rather, I'm learning. One can't waver from one's goal or one will never accomplish it."

Cody kicked a stone from the sidewalk. "I can't argue there." He looked over at her. "Are we at an impasse, Ellen?"

"We knew yesterday that we were. We knew it right off."

A rumble came from his throat. His eyes squinted. "I can't settle for an impasse. Nope. I won't."

The thudding in Ellen's heart had started to ease; now it began again. His words frightened her. They also thrilled her in a way she didn't want to be thrilled. Never before had she felt so much like a woman—a desirable woman. And to be desired by a man like this . . .

Her voice came, weak and cracking. "Just what do you expect then, Cody, if you won't accept things as they are?"

"I want you to stay in Shadow Valley."

Silence fell in step with them, a long silence, until she responded, "I see."

"I'm not a game-player, Ellen. I'm being honest. I have found you and I want to keep you. I want you to stay."

She cleared her throat. "Keep me?"

He winced. "Bad choice of words. What I really mean is, I just want us to have a chance. That's all. A chance."

"There is no chance," she whispered.

"It's a choice, damn it. You could stay."

"And you could leave...with me. Isn't that also within the realm of choices?"

His head jerked up. "New York? Good God. Don't even..." He paused. "How could I leave? I've invested everything I have here. There's no way I could leave Shadow Valley."

"And there's no way I can stay. I've invested everything, too, in my future."

"An uncertain future."

Anger gripped her. "Not uncertain at all. The only thing I'm certain of is that I don't belong here. If you knew this town better, you'd know why."

"I don't care why."

They were climbing the steep slope toward the truck-stop café. The red light was blinking brightly under the dark sky. Ellen thought, *Every moment with him is agony and every moment with him is magical. Like a magical dance in which they both knew the song and moved in its rhythm, while the words were being sung in a harsh and untranslatable foreign language. Words that didn't belong as they waltzed in the fallout of sun dust. Danced in the shadows of "never."* She felt like crying.

"Don't do this to me," she said.

"Don't do this to *me*," he answered.

Buster darted between them, chasing after a white butterfly that teased by dipping down and touching his black nose, then sailing off just out of his reach.

The butterfly reminded her of the white, floating ghost. Ellen wanted to grab Cody's arm and tell him about the misty figure of a woman that had enticed them with some eerie invitation to the mansion's dining room, and followed them, pursued them. She wanted to ask him what it meant.

But he wouldn't know. He couldn't. It was *her* dream, after all. *Her* message. Meredith might be right about the lure of the ghost, but even she couldn't figure out why.

Cody reached for her hand, which unnerved her because people passing by—people coming to and from the truck-stop café—would see them hand in hand. But she didn't pull away. Like in the dreams, she was afraid, on some deep level, to pull away.

"What are you thinking about?" he asked as they walked.

She turned. "Do you believe in ghosts?"

This took him by surprise. "Yeah."

"Do you? Why?"

He shrugged. "Millions of people all over the world claim to have seen them. Who am I to judge them and say they didn't? I think there is a spirit world around us and sometimes we get a glimpse of it."

"You haven't seen one yourself?"

"No. Why, Ellen? Are you still thinking about that dream you had?"

"Yes. The mansion. I saw the ghost in the window three different times when I was a kid."

"What does that have to do with you and me?"

"Nothing, I guess."

He cocked his head sideways to meet her eyes. "You dreamed about me and there was a ghost in the dream, and that concerns you. Why, Ellen?"

"Honestly, I don't know. Maybe it has to do with fear. The way you talk—about wanting me—frightens me a little." *It thrills me and frightens me at the same time.*

"I don't want to frighten you. You must never be afraid of me."

"I'm afraid of your . . . determination."

"You don't want me to want you?"

"No. I don't." *But I do!* The voice inside her screamed. *I've never wanted anything so much. I've never felt so much before . . . never thought about the woman inside me that trem-*

bles at your touch and wakens my senses into feeling what it's like to fall in love....

"You say no with tears in your voice, Ellen. Do you think I can't feel you tremble when I touch you? Do you think your eyes can wear a mask?"

BY EIGHT O'CLOCK that evening her customers at the truck-stop café were coming in with windblown hair and comments about the weather. Clouds had been gathering across the sky since midafternoon and the wind was picking up. Gramps was going to have his storm.

Ellen wasn't winning the struggle to throw off the weight of her anguish. Trying to keep away thoughts of Cody was like trying not to breathe. The vision of him attached itself stubbornly to her waking moments as well as her sleeping ones, and wouldn't let go.

Meredith's comments didn't help. Her friend wasn't about to let Ellen ignore the strange circumstances under which Cody walked into her life.

At nine o'clock Cody's incredibly resonant voice came on the radio with his nightly program of music and news. So even though he had not shown up at the café last night or tonight, Cody's presence was here just the same. His voice was haunting. It echoed from the very walls and drowned out all the other sounds.

There was just no way to forget yesterday's lunch. No way to erase the memory of the surprise on his face when she told him there would be no relationship. No way to forget how his eyes turned blue in the reflection of hers. But she had to forget, somehow. After the perfect, easy hours together, it had to end with this soft, aching memory—nothing more. Their lives were destined to go in opposite directions.

So they had said hello and they had said goodbye.

And still it didn't end. He returned in her dream. He showed up on the sidewalk to walk with her. His radio voice pervaded her world. Hard as it was to admit, Ellen watched the clock at work, anxious for his evening program to come on, when the vibrations of his beautiful voice overpowered her mind and took her back to the magic of her dreams. She couldn't get away from him. *Why did I have to meet you, Cody? Why do I have to want you?*

The sky blackened, threatening rain.

"Looks like we might be in for a bad one," one of the truckers drawled as he walked in from the parking lot holding on to his hat. A cool gust caught the door, forcing him to make a grab for the handle to pull it shut. There was a musty smell of rain in the wind.

"Then I'm moving on out," said another, digging into his pocket for his wallet. "I ain't got time to get delayed up here."

Grumbles of agreement preceded an exodus from the café. The drivers had deadlines to meet. Few of them ever stayed overnight in Shadow Valley because the Blue Spruce was lacking in overnight facilities. Before long, only local customers were left, some of whom were expressing concern about windows left open in their houses.

Ellen found herself worrying about her grandfather being home alone tonight. If he knew her uneasiness, he would scoff and remind her how many thousands of storms he had seen in his lifetime, and that in this part of the world, winter storms were the threat, not the summer rains of July. Still, he might worry that the upstairs windows were left open and try to navigate the stairs. His old body wasn't able to get up and down the stairway anymore.

Just before ten, the owner, Jed Mortimer, who was also the restaurant's evening cook, came out of the kitchen to check the sky from the front windows. The wind was blowing a sign back and forth, making curious plays of light on his unshaven face. "Millie planned to come in after her church program," he said. "But I phoned and left a message for her not to bother. Why don't you call it a night, Ellen? I just heard on the radio that this storm is blowing in pretty big and you'll want to get home before it starts to rain. I'll hold down the fort."

If any locals had been in the café, she'd be offered a ride down the hill, at least as far as the center of town. But Ellen didn't mind the walk. In fact, she didn't mind storms. The wind could be exhilarating.

Thunder began to rumble. "Thanks, I will go. I want to make sure Gramps is okay." She untied her apron and folded it carefully.

Jed Mortimer looked out at the sky again, but it was too dark to see anything. He said, "I'd have asked you to take off sooner, but back in the kitchen I didn't realize what the weather was doing."

She smiled. "It's just a nice summer storm, Jed. We need the rain. Gramps predicted it this morning. I should have listened to him and brought a scarf." She opened the door against the wind. "See you tomorrow."

6

IN HIS APARTMENT at the back of the radio station, Cody sat at his desk drinking a beer and sorting through bills. Or trying to. His head had begun to ache an hour ago, just after he'd signed off live with the storm warning. KUBS went off the air at ten every night, as it had for years, but he was developing programming that would continue until at least midnight. That was just the beginning of the plan he had for Shadow Valley. What the place needed was new blood. Young blood, to liven up the consciousness of the town and get some new revenue generated. An active radio station could make a big difference; it was the voice of the people. One step at a time, though; he'd just gotten here.

He tilted back in the chair, rocking recklessly. The dog raised his eyes as if to say, "Stop that. If you fall, the crash will disturb my rest."

"There's a storm coming in, Buster," Cody said. It amazed him that the dog didn't show the slightest reaction to the sound of rumbling thunder. The old Buster always tried to hide under a bed during a storm.

He threw down his pencil in frustration. "Damn, what's causing this headache? Thinking about Ellen all day would do it. Hell! Rejected before I even have a chance to prove to her what a great catch I am." The dog looked up quizzically. "I blew it, Buster. I let go of her."

Enraged, he got up to pour the rest of the beer down the sink. His chair crashed to the floor. He swore at it savagely and left it where it fell.

Agitation forced him to lie on the bed and close his eyes. The sounds of the electric storm roaring into Shadow Valley assailed his ears, making the pain worse. Wind screamed through the tops of pines. Giant bellows of thunder shook the house. Lightning slashed across the sky. Fog-drenched pictures tried to come through. Pictures from his childhood. Faint impressions of the house on Pebble Street. Apprehension. A sense of fear that wouldn't quite come clear. The storm was triggering images of a storm from his childhood, a certain storm. The memory was shrouded in confusion; he couldn't get it back. But the emotions were returning and threatening to make him sick.

As the storm gathered force outside, Cody's frustration grew. Lying down only made it worse. He sat up, impatiently shoving aside the guitar he had been playing earlier. His head dropped into his hands and he tried to hold it against the spinning.

A concerned Buster jumped up onto the bed and nuzzled against his friend's legs, lending support. Something was wrong and they both knew it.

Until now, it had been all right, returning home. A triumph, in fact. It felt great to conquer the past. But this storm was torching something deep inside him . . . reluming some smoldering ashes of the past. A thing unresolved was trying to surface, like the storm blowing up from some unknown source, with a need to express its own wild nature in the dark of night. Threatening danger. The storm had something to say to him. He had to listen to it. To feel it. To meet it. He had to meet it head-on, because the storm was danger!

"I have to go, Buster." He pushed the dog aside gently, and reached for his boots.

Lightning flashed outside the window seconds before a loud crack of thunder jarred the building. Buster's ears went back; he looked questioningly at the man.

Cody answered the dog's silent question. "I don't *know* why. I just know I have to go...."

It wasn't making any sense, being pulled by the force of an unseen memory. When he stood, the throbbing in his head got worse. The dog ran to stand by the door. Cody pulled on his waterproof windbreaker, saying as he zipped it, "Not this time, pal. You stay in where it's dry. I won't be out long." He pulled his rain hood up over his head.

By now the summer storm was in full force. Trees were swaying wildly and the bending branches seemed to be reaching down to grab him, as if in an attempt to shake him into awareness. In the howling of the wind he could hear voices, familiar voices from the past, but over the shrieking, he could recognize none of them. It was like living inside a hideous dream.

The nightmare! The storm was his nightmare! The one he had tried so hard to forget. As the storm's first raindrops hit his face, Cody headed blindly in the direction of the town center. He was following something, not knowing what. Streetlights, shining hoary and rain-blurred, served to guide the way through familiar darkness. Every step forward was like taking two steps backward, further and further into his past.

Desperately, he had wanted to forget the dream. Why was it so important now to remember it? What urgency was forcing him along the deserted main street, rushing him back in time through a raging storm?

Half a block away a silhouette appeared in the weak beam of a streetlamp, and at once he thought of Ellen. It couldn't be, and yet... and yet Ellen walked along this block every night on her way home from work. The small figure was hurrying, leaning into the wind and slashing rain. Cody's heart quavered, then lurched into panic.

He had been here before! She *had been here before, in a storm....*

Suddenly he remembered the danger of the wind! There wasn't much time!

Cody began to run. Tree branches whipped and swayed overhead, crashing and dancing together in rhythm with the wild wind—a loud and boisterous dance. Running, Cody glanced up at the tangled, lashing limbs of the huge trees, and he remembered.

"Ellen!" he shouted. "Get off the sidewalk!"

His voice was swallowed by the storm. He knew she could neither hear nor see him.

Lightning flashed, silvering the howling trees and rain-wet street for seconds and then the night went black again. In that flash he had seen the white of her blouse—just like before. Panic kicked in fully. He had to reach her in time! This time!

"Ellen!" Cody yelled again. But again his voice was lost against the howls of the forces of nature. Hurrying along the tree-lined sidewalk, Ellen didn't turn around.

A savage gust of wind nearly threw him off-balance. Cody could see her struggle against the wind, too, just as the terrible cracking sounded overhead. Recognizing the noise of a giant branch breaking, Cody, gasping for enough breath, reached Ellen in time to push her out of the path of the falling limb.

Or at least he hoped he had. The mass of wet leaves closing over him prevented him from seeing whether or not she was clear of the impact. A strike of searing pain hit him—the impact of the heavy limb across his back. He was aware of the weight, and then he was aware of nothing at all.

Ellen, startled by a forceful shove from behind, had let out a cry as she was sent tumbling toward the curb. A rush of terror gripped her, followed split seconds later by the crack of a branch breaking from a large old tree. Hard wet pavement rose up and smacked her painfully. She felt cold water soaking her blouse. Rivulets were running along the curb beneath her, and tentacles of dripping leaves—reaching from the fallen limb—trembled over her back.

Rain pelting her skin, Ellen picked herself up with difficulty. The dim streetlight outlined what she thought was the silhouette of a man lying facedown in the exact spot where she had been walking moments ago. The limb had fallen across his body! He was not moving. Gasping, she groped around in the dim light to separate branches in order to get closer to him.

Her eyes traveled up from the broad shoulders to his face, in profile, half hidden by leaves. Her heart lurched. *Cody! Cody* was the angel who had appeared out of the darkness to push her to safety and he'd been unable to get out of the way himself! How could this be? Why was he here, at this place, at this moment? *And why wasn't he stirring?*

Ellen cried out his name. She made a frantic attempt to lift the limb and couldn't budge it. Tears of panic welled up and spilled out, mixing with the rain on her face. *Surely he couldn't be dead!*

On hands and knees she clawed at the leafy branch, trying to reach him. Finally, she could touch his face. His eyes were closed. He seemed to be breathing. Ellen tried to calm herself, tried to think. Precious time was being wasted! She had to get help!

The police station! Brushing her hair from her eyes, she could see light in the window of the red brick building half a block away on the opposite side of the street.

The storm was raging by now, rain pounding down and the wind screaming. Ellen struggled to disentangle herself from the horizontal arms of leaves. She felt as if she was moving in slow motion.

Finally free, she looked back desperately. How could she leave him lying there alone? Damn it, she had no choice! Sobs of fear assailed her as she took off running. The light in the window seemed to get smaller instead of larger. Her head throbbed with the panic. *Why wasn't Cody moving? Was he just knocked out because the branch had hit his head? Could it have broken his back? Could he die, lying there alone?* Someone had to get him out, and fast!

The rain-swept streets were slick. Twice she lost her balance trying to run at full speed against the relentless wind.

Her feet slipped again on the steps of the building. A sharp stab of pain went through her wrist when she caught herself. Her shin slammed into the cement step. Finally she was opening the door and rushing into the musty, brightly-lit lobby. No one sat at the desk, but, to her relief, two uniformed officers were standing in the back of the room smoking and discussing some papers on a clipboard. She knew them both—Mark Dickens and Joe Garry. They looked up in alarm to see Ellen standing in the doorway soaked to the skin, her hair in her eyes, and panic on her face.

"There's been an accident!" she exclaimed. "A man is trapped under a fallen tree and he's unconscious!"

Joe Garry smothered his cigarette in an ashtray. "Where?"

She waved her hand. "On Main Street, outside the furniture store. It might take two men to lift that tree. I don't know how badly he's hurt. Hurry!"

The taller man, Mark Dickens, grabbed rain slickers from hooks near the door. He was already half into one while he handed another to his partner and a third to Ellen. "Here. You need this."

"I'll be right behind you," Joe said. "I'll put through a call for an ambulance."

Ellen was already out the door and running. Mark caught up with her easily, and was soon well ahead. He had been a track star in school, she recalled; he could outrun anybody in town. She had covered only half the distance when she saw that Mark had reached the scene of the accident. By that time, Joe Garry was right behind her.

In the whipping wind, the two young men lifted the heavy branch. An ambulance arrived from the hospital only three blocks away. Ellen stepped back into the shadows and watched as paramedics in yellow rain slickers bent over Cody's motionless form. They didn't turn him over. In driving rain, they lifted him into the ambulance.

She rushed up as they were closing the doors. "How badly is he hurt?"

"Can't tell," one of the men replied. "We'll have to examine him at the hospital."

What other response could she expect? At least Cody was alive! She fought down the urge to jump into the ambulance and stood in the streetlight shaking so hard her legs would scarcely hold her up.

Mark Dickens stood beside her. "Lucky you saw it, Ellen. Where were you when this happened? Do you know who the guy is?"

Her voice sounded weak against the wind. "Cody Laird. He's new here. He owns the radio station. I don't know what happened, for sure. I was walking home from work. I heard the noise of the tree breaking and somebody pushed me from behind. I fell, and when I got up, I saw that it had fallen on him."

They were walking back in the direction of the police station.

Joe said, "I'll get a car and go on over to the hospital for a report."

Ellen turned. "I'll go with you."

Some ten minutes later she and the officer, both wearing dripping police raincoats, were standing in the reception area of the county hospital. Ellen was grateful Joe was there because without him, getting information would be more difficult.

He said, "You're soaking wet, Ellen. You must be freezing."

"I'm numb from being so scared."

"You say the guy was behind you?"

"Yes, but I didn't know it. He must have seen the branch break, although I don't see how he could. It all happened at once. Do you think the branch broke his back?"

"It's possible, but I doubt it." The officer unbuttoned his coat and reached into his shirt pocket for his cigarettes and a lighter. "If that limb had landed on you, small as you are, it might have killed you."

"I know. And it would have hit me—I was right under it."

He rested a hand on her shoulder. "You're shaking like a leaf. You ought to go home and get dry."

"How can I until I know how badly hurt he is?"

Taking a hard puff, Joe Garry blew out a mouthful of smoke. The nurse at the desk in the far corner of the room glared at his cigarette, but didn't say anything, perhaps because he was in uniform and on duty. "This might take a while, though. Why don't I run you home and wait for you to change into something dry, and we'll get back here before the doctor is ready to tell us anything."

She thought this over and nodded gratefully. "I can change in five minutes."

DURING THEIR WAIT in the hospital lounge, Ellen decided to telephone the Calhouns.

Meredith answered.

"It's me," Ellen breathed, wishing she didn't have to take time to explain. "I'm at the hospital. Cody was hurt when a broken tree branch—"

"What? Hey, slow down, Ellen!"

"I'm calling to find out if Jeff knows anything about Cody's family—where they might be . . . anyone to contact. I know you said you didn't think he knew anything, but I had to ask anyhow, just in case."

"This sounds serious!" Meredith's voice had risen several octaves.

"It might be. Is Jeff—?"

"He isn't here. He went out to the country on a call and he's staying over rather than drive home in this storm. Hey, are you okay? You sound fragmented."

"I'm fine."

"Should I come?"

"You can't do that."

"Hell, I can if you need me."

Ellen's voice softened. "Joe Garry is with me. He's on duty. I'm okay, really. I doubt if Jeff would know Cody's family, I just thought I'd give it a try."

"Ellen, the dreams were some kind of warning, just as I thought. The ghost was a messenger of doom. Maybe that was her connection to Cody . . . or maybe it's the ghost's revenge—"

"Meredith, will you stop! It was an accident."

"Oh, really? Just a plain accident? Or is there something you're not telling me?"

Ellen swallowed hard, feeling the weakness in her knees. There was deep concern and worry in Meredith's voice. Ellen felt the comfort of having one friend in Shadow Valley who truly cared. Even if she tended to be a cheerleader of the occult and sometimes a peddler of doom.

"I can't talk about it now," Ellen said. "I know very little at this point, but I promise to phone later and let you know how he is."

Another thirty minutes passed before Cody was moved from the emergency room into intensive care and Joe was able to talk to the doctor. Dr. Tribble was an elderly man with a gray mustache, whom Ellen had seen around town all her life but had never spoken with. Dressed in jeans and a sweat-shirt, her hair still damp, she stood beside the police officer so Dr. Tribble wouldn't question her right to be there. Joe, acting official, took out his pad and pencil to add the medi-cal prognosis to his accident report.

"Multiple injuries," the doctor said. "A bad blow to the head, three bruised ribs, one cracked rib—internal injuries. So far, no sign of regaining consciousness. We're watching him closely for concussion for the next few hours." He turned to Ellen. "Are you a relative?"

Ellen scarcely heard the question. "No. A friend. He has no relatives in Shadow Valley."

"We'll need some personal information. Has anyone taken information from you?"

She shook her head. "No, and I really can't give you any. I barely know him."

"Give us what you can, then."

"No spinal injuries?" she asked.

"Not that we can determine, nor skull fracture. He'll be all right unless the head injury causes complications." The doc-tor turned to the police officer, ignoring Ellen. "Is that all you need?"

"Yeah." Joe nodded. "Can we see him?"

"There's no point. He isn't conscious."

Joe sensed how much she wanted to see Cody. He had tried, and for that Ellen was grateful. He suspected Cody was more to her than a casual friend. Strange, she thought. Joe had never been her friend; he was just a guy from school who would classify her as one of the Pebble kids. They had never held a conversation before tonight. Yet he had gone out of his way to be nice to her. Was it because it was his duty as a police officer? No, it had gone beyond that. He had been sincerely helpful.

Now he turned to her and asked if she wanted a lift home after she had filled out what she could of the admission forms.

"Thanks," she replied. "But I think I'll stay, just in case there's some change."

"Why not get some sleep and check back first thing in the morning? Maybe he'll be awake by morning." Joe Garry smiled. "You can't thank him until he wakes up, Ellen."

She shrugged. "Maybe you're right."

"Sure I am. My experience around here has taught me that they won't give you any information about a patient unless you're his spouse or his mother. And these chairs can get damned hard after a while."

Rubbing her wrist, Ellen glanced at the closed doors behind which Cody lay unconscious, his immediate fate in the hands of professionals in white uniforms. There was something strange, all right. *How could he have been behind her on the sidewalk, without her seeing him? Why was he there, in the storm?* More was going on than she understood.

Please wake up soon, Cody, she pleaded in silence. *Please be all right and wake up and explain to me what is happening....*

7

THE RAIN-WASHED MORNING air absorbed the scent of pine. Dazzling sunshine moved down and across the narrow valley as the last of the clouds thinned and scattered. The gentle calm of day gave no hint of the fury of last night's winds, but the light revealed the damage—fallen branches, blown debris, moving brown water rippling along the curbs, leaf-capped puddles.

As she walked briskly from home toward the hospital, Ellen was grateful for the sunlight, for the darkness of the night had seemed to go on forever. On Main Street, the giant felled bough had been cleared away, but scattered leaves remained. The broken tree stood forlornly lopsided. Shuddering, she hurried past it, trying to will away the memory of Cody trapped there.

Minutes later Ellen stood at his bedside, gazing down at his pale face. Although he had been moved in the early morning to a private room, he had not regained consciousness, and this frightened her. He appeared to be sleeping, unaware of the IV needle taped in his arm.

"Cody?" she whispered, leaning close. "Please wake up."

Stripes of thin light slanted in through the vertical window blinds, falling across the white sheets of his bed. There were echoes through the corridors, and the smell of disinfectant. Disoriented, Ellen sat on the bedside chair, her hand touching his, and studied every line of his body under the thin white blanket, and every detail of his face under a shadow of beard. Dark hair curled over his forehead. His features were nearly perfect; he was beautiful.

"Cody, who are you?" she whispered. "How have you haunted my dreams before I ever knew you? How have you invaded my every thought since I met you? Why were you there last night?"

Throughout the morning, she moved only when asked to by someone ministering to him, and then returned to her vigil.

Before noon, Jeff Calhoun came in, looking hassled and a little surprised to see her. "I got your message, Ellen. What happened?" He studied the still form in the bed.

"A freak accident," she answered unsteadily. "He was under the tree just as the storm took off a branch. I thought you might know his family."

"No . . ." He frowned. "I didn't realize you two knew each other."

"We don't, very well."

Calhoun leaned over Cody. "Concussion, the doctor said. I'm sure he'll be okay, but I wish he'd wake up." He checked his watch. "I have a patient scheduled for surgery." He was looking at her curiously, probably wondering why she was standing vigil. "When he comes to, tell him I was here, will you? And that I'll be back."

An hour later Cody began to stir, turning his head painfully. Ellen straightened. "Cody, can you hear me?"

After what seemed a long time, his eyes fluttered open and he looked up at her dazedly. His lips formed her name. "Ellen?"

Thank God you're awake! She gripped his hand firmly. "You were trapped under a tree branch. Do you remember?"

Cody frowned, closed his eyes and then opened them again. She realized he must be in pain; of course, he would be. She must get someone—

"It was a dream," he rasped.

Ellen bent toward him. "I wish it were. It can't be feeling much like a dream right now."

"It was a dream," he repeated and closed his eyes against rising awareness of the pain. Perspiration was beginning to show on his forehead and another weak attempt to move made him wince.

He's delirious, she thought, as tears welled in her eyes. Ellen swallowed as if that would hold the tears back. *Stay in control!* she scolded herself as she rose from the chair. "I'm going to find your doctor . . . who will be very pleased to see you've decided to wake up."

His eyes remained tightly closed against the pain; he didn't try to look at her again.

Afterward, they wouldn't let her see him. Ellen paced around the waiting room drinking coffee. The image of Cody's glazed eyes was burned into her consciousness. Surely he couldn't really have thought he was dreaming—not when he awoke in so much pain.

A nurse approached, looking baffled. "Ellen Montrose?"

"Yes. Is something wrong?"

"There's a telephone call for you from Germany."

"What?"

The woman shrugged in amazement. "From Stuttgart. I could barely understand the operator. She asked for you by name."

Ellen cleared her throat to keep from smiling and followed the woman to the phone.

"*Bitte, ist das eine Fraulein?*"

Ellen glanced at the nurse and lowered her voice out of her hearing. "*Ja. So?*"

"*Ach,* I had to know," Meredith answered in a strong German accent. How is the boy?"

"Barely awake. With a very bad headache, I think."

"But he'll live."

"I'm sure of it."

"Good. Then I can ask the rest. What the devil is going on? I threw the runes last night after you called and this thing about a third party came up. A reference to your ghost, I'm sure. We need to go out there, Ellen. To the mansion. You're being called there for some reason." Meredith's voice was so soft, Ellen had trouble hearing. But this was to be expected because she was phoning from Jeff's office; Ellen could hear faint barking in the background. "I think we need to confront this spook and find out what it's up to."

Ellen glanced toward the nurse. "I think you may be right about going out there to the mansion after all the dreams about it."

"Vee must, *meine kleine Freunde. Und* soon. Soon. *Auf Wiedersehen.*"

Ellen hung up with a shudder. Meredith meant for them to go *inside.* They had prowled around the grounds countless times over the years, but had never thought of *breaking in.* Ellen's head swam. At least a thousand times she had pictured the inside of that house. That girl, Carolyn, had described it as magnificent. Other kids, including Meredith, thought she was embellishing to show off, but Ellen wanted to believe it was as resplendent as Carolyn's stories implied.

Seconds after she had hung up the phone, it rang again. She picked it up on the first ring. "Hello?"

"Is he conscious?" Meredith asked in her own voice.

"Just barely. He's in a lot of pain."

"I wanted to warn you. Don't kiss him when he is unconscious or asleep. It's monstrously bad luck to do that."

"Oh, Mere! For heaven's sake!"

"Deadly serious. The gypsy told me. To kiss an unconscious man is very bad luck. Oh, I know you claim not to be superstitious. I also know you respect my infinite wisdom in these matters."

"I don't know why you'd think I'd kiss him, anyhow."

"It's just a precautionary comment, that's all. How long are you going to be hanging around there?"

"Until I know he's really all right, I suppose."

"Just don't get carried away and kiss him."

The nurse wouldn't let her back into Cody's room, but assured her he was just undergoing tests. Not to worry.

I'll worry if I damned well please, Ellen thought. No one else was here to worry about him, no one else to care. Cody wasn't alone, though. He did have someone—he had her.

The noon hour came and went. She was due at the truck stop at two. She couldn't hang around here keeping chairs warm when she had to be at work. Reluctantly, Ellen left the hospital, scarcely feeling the sunshine when it touched her face.

At the café, co-workers and customers were talking about last night's accident. Everyone assumed the two of them had been together; what else could they think? And Ellen could hardly admit it wasn't true, so she said nothing. The wrist she'd twisted on the steps of the police station hurt every time she lifted a heavy plate. The radio was a constant distraction—the station was playing a tape of a previously recorded show. All Ellen could think about was seeing him again.

She returned home to a dark house. Her grandfather was not in bed, but sitting at the front window staring out at the stars.

"I am tired, my Ellen," he said softly.

She joined him at the window, sliding an arm affectionately around his thin waist. "Then why aren't you in bed, Gramps?"

He turned his head and smiled wistfully. "I am another kind of tired." His hand came to rest on hers. "Do you believe in angels, darlin'? In guardian angels?"

She swallowed. "Yes. I most certainly do."

"And so you should, for they are real."

They sat side by side in the dark, looking up at the night sky. Her heart was filled with love. And trepidation. After a long silence, she asked, "Why did you ask about the angels?"

Again the smile softened his weathered face. "I have heard them singing these nights."

Tears sprang to her eyes.

His hand rose gently in protest. "It's fine music, not sad. Actually, it's a good song to dance to, that's what I think. Dancing with the angels, now that'll be a kick."

She lowered her head sideways, against his shoulder, and whispered, "You don't feel good lately, do you, Gramps?"

"I told you, I'm just tired. I miss your grandmother. She's waiting for me, you know."

"Yes. I know."

"Nothin' to cry about."

Her arm tightened around him. "I love you, Gramps."

IN THE MORNING, HE WAS out working in the garden when Ellen opened her window. She wondered if he had slept at all, but wouldn't ask. Her grandfather deserved the dignity of not being fussed over like a frail old man. He was in control of his life, had always been, and he had taught her to take control, too. It was the most valuable lesson she had ever learned.

No more was said about last night. After an earlier-than-usual breakfast, he took to his favorite chair to read, and Ellen, wearing a crisp white blouse and flowered cotton skirt and sandals, set out for the hospital.

SHE CLUTCHED HER SMALL handbag, feeling the pounding of her heart as she entered his room. Cody lay on his back with his eyes closed. As if he sensed a presence, his eyes slowly opened.

"You're awake," she said barely above a whisper.

"I'd rather not be." His voice was raspy.

She winced. "Cody... how can I thank you for what you did, pushing me out of the way? You were hurt saving me."

He gazed up at her. "You're okay?"

"Yes. But you're not. You're in a lot of pain."

"It was a dream..." he said.

This again? She leaned closer. "You lying here in that hospital bed is *not* a dream. As much as I wish it were. The truth is that I probably owe my life to you. I don't understand where you came from, in the storm."

As if it hurt to move a single muscle of his body, he lay still, not welcoming conversation, his breathing labored. She felt she ought to let him rest.

Cody moved his hand to find hers and grasped it tightly. "I dreamed it, Ellen—the storm, you, the branch breaking above you.... It's how I knew...."

She sucked in her breath. "You dreamed about the storm before it happened?"

"Yeah..."

"But how could—?" Ellen's voice halted. She shook her head in confusion. "You told me you never remember dreams."

His grasp remained strong, despite the weakness of his voice. "I don't. The storm made it come back...somehow. I knew you were in danger...."

"You dreamed about the branch?"

He nodded slightly—all he could manage with the headache.

Ellen wanted to blurt out, *And I dreamed about you before I met you! Why? What forces are playing with us in our sleep?* Trying to keep her voice calm, for his sake, she asked, "You dreamed it the night before?"

"No. A long time ago."

"How long?"

He winced. "My ribs are killing me. Every breath hurts. I don't know why they're so damned stingy with the morphine...."

Ellen fought back tears, because her tears would only make things worse. She asked, "Shall I get a nurse?"

"Anybody with a needle will do." His breath came in a ragged moan. "Threaten them if you have to."

She pulled her cold hand away from the grip of his hot one and turned toward the door just as a nurse entered with pain medication and asked Ellen to step out.

Had he been hurt in his dream? Did people feel pain in dreams? She returned five minutes later when the nurse left. Cody was already breathing easier. She asked, "Better?"

He didn't open his eyes. "I'm getting sleepy."

"Sleepy is good. Is there anything you need before I go?"

"Will you explain the situation to Buster?"

"Oh! Buster! Where is he?"

"At the station. Make sure they're taking—"

"Taking care of him. Sure. Don't worry."

Ellen gazed at his pale, unshaven face, hoping he hadn't yet drifted into sleep. "How long ago?" she asked.

"Hmm?"

"You said you had the dream a long time ago. A week? A month? How long?"

His eyes remained closed, his breathing unchanged. He wet his lips with his tongue and muttered, groggily, "I was twelve."

"What? You don't mean twelve years old?"

"Yeah . . ."

"But—" Ellen stopped herself. He was too sleepy to talk. Was he confused because of the strong drugs? she wondered. No, he had said twelve because he meant twelve. *But what could a dream Cody had at the age of twelve have to do with her?*

She studied the still form in the bed, and his handsome face. Cody was helpless in sleep, his strong hands were limp, his thoughts no longer cunning. She wondered what he had been like as a little boy, innocent in sleep. There was nothing innocent about this man . . . and yet, Ellen felt a strong desire to take care of him, hold him, take his pain away.

A tear found its way down her cheek. "Cody. . ." she muttered. "Cody . . . who are you? Why do I love you?" With the tears moist on her face, Ellen bent over him and touched her lips to his forehead, then his mouth. A soft kiss.

Only afterward, walking away from the sterile environment of the hospital, did Ellen remember Meredith's warning.

As anxious as she was to try to talk to him again, Ellen didn't return in the afternoon because Cody needed to sleep. Instead, she spent an hour trying to find Buster, then saw to it that he had food and water. *Lucky I'm not superstitious*, Ellen told herself every time she thought about the kiss. Each time she said it, an unfamiliar fear would surface.

THE FOLLOWING MORNING Cody was more receptive to company. He was awake and alert, clean-shaven, and listening to a small radio that sat on the bedside table. But he lay quite still, guarding against the pain in his ribs.

Ellen entered his room wearing a pale yellow sundress with pearl buttons to match the pearls at her throat. She smiled. "I found your dog sniffing at the very spot where you got hurt."

Cody smiled. "I guess he sensed something was wrong." He gestured toward the table. "Would you turn off the radio?"

She did, saying, "You look much better than yesterday."

"That isn't saying much. I feel like hell."

Ellen drew a chair close to the bed and sat down. "Cody, I'm so sorry this happened. I've already thanked you for saving my life, but I'm not sure you remember, so I must thank you again. If it weren't for me, you wouldn't be in the hospital."

His gray-blue eyes, lucid now, looked up into hers. "There's nothing to thank me for. I'm just glad I had the forewarning."

"The dream, you mean."

"The dream came several times over a period of months when I was twelve. I had forgotten until the storm began to trigger the memory. I knew I had to go out in it, but I didn't remember why until I heard the branch creak."

Ellen wondered if the blow to his head might have affected his memory and he had only imagined a long-ago dream. "You said there was a girl—"

"I know she was you."

"Come on. You lived in Denver. You didn't know me."

Cody gazed at her with an expression she had never seen. "I've been lying here thinking about it for hours. I'm sure it was you. In the dream you were a kid, too. And yes, I must have known you, Ellen. I didn't live in Denver. I grew up here."

She gave a start. "In Shadow Valley?"

He nodded. "I lived in a house at the end of Pebble Street, the one with the round windows under the eaves."

Ellen could only mutter, "Pebble Street?"

He stirred restlessly, moving his legs under the blanket, wincing with the discomfort in his ribs. "You would have been only eight when I was twelve. But I would have seen you with the other kids. I knew it was you who was in danger."

Tightness constricted her throat. "The house at the end of the street where Buster lived . . . Oh, I . . . I do remember you now! You had Buster and a black-and-yellow bike and . . ." She paused, confused. "Why don't I remember your name?"

"Because I was Kevin Reilly then. I changed my name when I went to Denver with the band."

The blood drained from her face. Kevin Reilly? She did remember Kevin Reilly but would never have made the connection. She could scarcely make it now. She gazed at him, awestruck. "Once you chased away some kids who were taunting me on the way home from school. They were calling me names and you rescued me. Oh, not because you knew me. It was because I was one who belonged to your world—Pebble Street—and I couldn't defend myself. You knew. . . ." Her eyes glazed with painful memories.

Cody recognized the look. "Yeah, sure I knew. But I don't remember the incident you're talking about."

"You wouldn't. It was just one of a thousand scrapes you were into all the time. You big kids were so mean and always in fights. But I thought for years about it, how you defended me. I pretended you secretly liked me."

He smiled. "It must have been true, even though I was occupied with being tough and worldly, and you were—"

"One of the insignificant little kids," she interjected.

He nodded. "Nevertheless, it must have been true that I noticed you and liked you, or why else would I have had the dream? It was the nightmare I told you about. Scared me to death because it was so real. The girl under the tree. The storm. The branch tearing off the tree and hitting her."

"It hit her?"

"Yeah. It's as vivid as if I'd dreamed it yesterday. I rushed up to warn her and the branch fell on us both. I thought it was how I was going to die." He reached up and rubbed his forehead thoughtfully. "It's crazy! A dream comes true sixteen years later! I don't know what to make of it."

"It's very strange...."

"More than you know, Ellen. Something about the storm really tugged at me and forced me out into it. I knew there was danger. I saw you in the streetlight and remembered."

Ellen was tempted to tell him she, too, had dreamed of him before they met, but he wasn't well enough to hear it! It had been difficult enough telling him she didn't want a relationship. Now, her pulling away made even less sense. Those dreams meant something; she knew it. But what?

"Cody," she began carefully. "Were you ever inside the Whitfield mansion?"

"No. Were you?"

"Only in my imagination and my dreams."

"And I was in there with you, in your dream." He smiled. "I'm flattered that you'd dream about me. It's a good sign. It means I have been in your thoughts."

For a dozen years? I hardly think so. Ellen bit her lip. Obviously, mention of the mansion had no effect on him, wasn't important to him, so he had no connection with it. How could he, anyway? A kid from Pebble Street ...

There had to be some way to keep him from dominating her thoughts—waking and sleeping. To try to set her world back upright again. To focus on her lifelong plans. Pain stabbed at her heart each time she thought about never seeing Cody again. She forced away the thought and touched his limp hand. "There's so much I don't understand," she whispered. *My own feelings included.* "I want you to get well and get out of here."

A silence fell over the room, filled only by the sounds of the hospital—a tray clanking somewhere in the hallway and a muffled summons for a doctor on a loudspeaker. And the sound of Cody's breathing, shallow breaths against his bandaged ribs.

She whispered, "Are you all right?"

"I will be soon. Don't worry about me, Ellen."

"Is there a lot of pain?"

"I said not to worry."

His voice had lost some of the strength it had earlier, and his eyes were not as bright. "You're getting tired," she said. "All this conversation is taking your energy. You need to sleep. I don't want to make it worse by being here."

"You could never make anything worse." His eyes closed.

Ellen's sigh shook with deep inner pain she scarcely understood. "I'm going to let you rest. I'll see you tomorrow."

THROUGH THE DISTRACTIONS of the day, thoughts of Cody's kindness worked their way into her consciousness. While stopping by the station with a box of dog biscuits for Buster . . . while making her grandfather's favorite vegetable soup . . . while waiting on her customers, thoughts of Cody pushed through. He was lying in a hospital because of her, because he cared. His caring overwhelmed her.

She was taking an order when Cody's taped voice came over the radio again. At the sound of his voice, tears filled her eyes. A new kind of longing gripped her—a longing for the way she felt when she was with him.

Ellen took a bag of homemade cookies from the café and stopped by the hospital on her way home from work. The corridors were deserted at that time of night, long past visiting hours, and the sole nurse at the desk allowed her to go in "for a moment."

Cody was asleep. Trembling, Ellen gazed down at him, studying his handsome face in the light from the hallway, remembering the secret kiss she had given him, remembering her embarrassment over her runaway emotions just hearing the sound of his voice on the radio. *What's happening?* her heart cried out. *What's happening to me? If it's love, love hurts....*

Quietly she set the bag of cookies on the table and bent to kiss his forehead as she had done before. If it was bad luck, the damage had already been done. If she could have held him in her arms while he slept, she would have. If he didn't know...

"Sleep peacefully," she whispered. "I'll see you in the morning." Ellen couldn't know in that quiet moment that tomorrow she wouldn't be seeing him at all.

8

CODY DRIFTED INTO SLEEP thinking about her. She seemed so close and so distant at the same time. He felt her touch, like in a dream.

Deep in the night, his dream took shape.

The old Whitfield mansion on the hill looked younger than its years as he, wearing a tuxedo, wandered up from the gate and entered through the front door without knocking. As if he were expected there.

In a gold and pink foyer, from which the stair curled upward, he was aware of something lurking in the shadows and knew the house was haunted. He couldn't see a spirit being, but he could feel its chill.

More curious than frightened, he walked through a white-pillared archway into a candlelit dining room. A woman in a pale blue gown stood with her back to the door. She turned suddenly. Ellen! The instant he saw her, he knew he had been in this mansion before, with her, though he couldn't recall when.

The woman he knew he loved walked toward him slowly, smiling, as if she had been expecting him. Her gown rustled like distant music. Dancing candle flames shone on her pale hair and caught the brilliance of her sparkling earrings. Her face was radiant—she was more radiant than he had ever seen her. When he was close enough to look into her eyes, he could see a reflection of himself.

Something heavy came down on his shoulder. Instantaneously, he believed it was the ghost whose presence had been

*so strong in the mansion—the ghost trying to prevent him
from getting close enough to Ellen to touch her. A light shone
in his eyes....*

A woman's voice—not the wail of a discarnate spirit—
startled him.

"Wake up. Time for your medication."

He forced open his eyes, furious that the dream had been
interrupted. No light was showing through the window
blinds. "What the hell time is it?"

"A quarter to five." The nurse didn't smile as she pushed
up his sleeve and swabbed his arm with cold alcohol.

After the injection, there was no point in trying to go back
to sleep. He would soon be disturbed again for the morning
hospital rituals. Besides, his mind was whirling and heavy
with what he had been seeing before he woke. That
dream . . . it was vaguely familiar, as if he had dreamed it before.

Cody lay watching the sky gradually begin to lighten outside the window, unable to let go of the magical sensations
of the dream.

It was then, still floating in the magic, that he realized it was
the first time he had remembered a dream since shutting out
the dream of his death in the storm. That storm had broken
the seal on his dreams! He could remember again. And he remembered Ellen looking at him in a way she never had in the
"real" world.

Maybe someday, he mused in the gray hospital room,
maybe someday she would understand the way he felt. Hell,
even *he* didn't understand the way he felt. He only knew he
loved her. He felt certain he had dreamed of her—not just last
night but before. And in the dreams he loved her. Long ago.

ELLEN TOSSED RESTLESSLY, tried to get back to sleep and
couldn't. What had wakened her so suddenly at a quarter to

five in the morning? The house was still and the birds hadn't yet begun their wake-up concert. Yet something had pulled her abruptly out of a fine and lovely dream.

The mansion again. The candles in the dining room were lit and Cody had appeared in the doorway. He was dressed in a tuxedo as if for a special celebration.

When she walked closer to him, she could see in his eyes the reflection of herself. Then something bright shone in her eyes—something she couldn't identify in the silence of the night.

She lay for a time in the dark, until fear began to creep over her. Something was wrong! The house was unnaturally still. It was always still at five in the morning, but this was different now. Deeper than silence, the house felt more empty than it had ever been.

With an urgent cry, Ellen shot out of bed and rushed down the stairs. Before she entered her grandfather's room, she summoned enough willpower to stop herself.

"There is no need to panic," she told her rigid body and her pumping heart. "He wouldn't want you to panic. Just remember, Gramps wanted to leave and he was ready." She remembered he had told her the angels had been coming to him in the night. . . .

FOUR DAYS LATER, in the afternoon, a thick cover of clouds hung low over the valley, threatening rain. *Why couldn't there be sunshine to say goodbye in?* Ellen wondered, as she wrapped a dark sweater around her shoulders. But Gramps had never minded bleak skies.

What Emory Leo Montrose hadn't liked was ceremony. He had pointedly instructed his granddaughter that his service be a simple one, for although the family had been in Shadow Valley since the silver mine opened in 1880, there were very few of the old miners left, and they were tough old men who

had finished with tradition long ago. Ellen and her grandfather had kept mostly to themselves in the ten years since her
grandmother died. Like Cody, she had lost her father in a
mine accident—the same mine accident. Her mother had run
away from Pebble Street and died in a Denver charity hospital. She, like Cody, was the last of the line. He might go on
remembering the stories of the mining days; she would not.
Not after today.

Maybe she should have told Cody about her grandfather
so he'd understand why she hadn't been back to see him, but
there had been so much to do. And Cody had problems
enough of his own right now. When Ellen thought about it
after the fact, she realized neither of these reasons was valid.
If she were honest with herself, she had to admit she just
hadn't had the strength to deal with the emotional overload.
No one understood how it was between her and Gramps. Her
grief wasn't something she wanted to share with Cody or
anyone. So she hadn't been to see him, and he would wonder why.

At the graveside the preacher's voice droned on as a light
wind blew in scattered raindrops from the mountaintops. A
dozen neighbors gathered around, but Ellen scarcely felt the
presence of any except the mysterious small figure with a veil
over her face, wearing gloves to hide her diamond rings. *In
this whole town I have only one friend and she is in disguise . . . always in disguise.* Meredith was here, and for that
Ellen was grateful.

Gramps had left and his love was gone with him, and with
Meredith so silent, behind the veil, Ellen had never felt so
alone. Under the shade trees, a shadow suddenly fell over her,
and the shadow was strangely warm, familiar.

Before she could turn, he moved in close and took her
hand. At his caring touch, the weight of loneliness light-
ened.

What was he doing out of the hospital? Ellen had assumed he wouldn't be discharged for another couple of days. He must have come straight from his hospital bed! She could feel the love in the warmth of his hand, comforting her. It was impossible not to love this man. *I do love him, I can't help it. . . . I love him terribly and helplessly.*

Cody said nothing but stood very close, his shoulder against hers. His silence was saying, "I'm here for you. Lean on me."

When the others had offered their condolences, Meredith stepped up to take Ellen's hand, a silent gesture of love. Through the veil she looked up at Cody, fixing her gaze on him. He stared back, and their eyes locked in an expression of curiosity. A glint of understanding came into his eyes; he saw what no one else in Shadow Valley knew.

Words were unnecessary. Meredith gave Ellen a tender hug and backed away. She disappeared as silently as she had come.

The two of them stood alone at the grave site listening to the song of a warbling bird. He asked, "Are you okay?"

"That was my first question to you, Cody. You must have just been discharged."

He smiled. "I discharged myself."

She studied his eyes, which were darker than usual under the clouds. "Was that wise?"

"Sure it was. I thought I might be needed. I wanted to be here for you."

Ellen looked at the ground because it was hard to look at him. Only someone from Pebble Street would have realized how alone she would be, out here, because of cutting herself off from the rest of the town. Her grandfather's death had been kept as quiet as possible because he would have wanted it that way, and so did she. Most people wouldn't understand. Cody would.

He walked with Ellen across the soft green lawn, past cold and silent stones, through the barred metal gate, and onto the road. On the hill behind them, dark against the sky, stood the Whitfield mansion. She noticed Cody looking up at it curiously and wondered if he was thinking of the dream she had told him about—of the two of them in that big old house. It wouldn't do at all to tell him it was only one dream of many, or that the dreams were becoming more vivid. "Thank you," she said as they walked.

"For what?"

"For being here."

His only response was to take her hand protectively.

Their footsteps crunched softly on the surface of the gravel road. Rain-threatening clouds that had been playing dancing games in the sky all day slid lower. Ellen said, "Your ribs are still bandaged, I assume."

He looked at the sky. "You're afraid if we get caught in the rain, the bandage will get soaked and soggy?"

"And you'd have to have it replaced."

He grinned. "I'd just take it off and dry it and you could wrap it back on."

His suggestion brought a flush to Ellen's cheeks. The thought of seeing his body—touching his body—caused unwelcome tingling sensations in areas of her own that had been numb for a very long time, perhaps always.

"I'd be too afraid of hurting you," she said, vaguely aware that the statement was about more than wrapping on a bandage. It was about the deep, trembling needs of her body and her heart, and the temptation to succumb to those needs. The intense and fluctuating emotions of the past few days had left her vulnerable and confused and intensely aware of needs within her that had been so long denied. Cody's strength and his nearness were as welcome as sunshine shining through a bank of gray clouds.

And he knew it.

"I wouldn't worry about your touch hurting me," he said.

She had to think back to what they had been talking about. *Oh, the bandage.* "Cody, how do you really feel? Be honest. You're not walking with your usual casual stride."

He glanced over at her. "I've had a cracked rib before. They heal. My concern is how you feel."

"I'm all right. Gramps prepared both of us for his leaving."

They walked in silence to the end of the gravel road and the entrance to Pebble Street. Ellen knew he was walking home with her and didn't try to stop him, even though she had never let anyone, ever before, walk her to her home. It was different now. Everything was different. Even the birds sounded different on Pebble Street. The shade trees cast wider shadows. The paint-chipped houses looked more bleak and forlorn than ever. What might have been silence was filled with the echoes of the past; she didn't want to go home alone.

On the narrow porch, gazing at the carefully tended flowers in the front yard, he waited for her to unlock the door.

"Do you want to come in? I'll make us some coffee."

He nodded, glad she wasn't going to be stubborn enough to insist on being alone at a time when she needed somebody.

The neatness of the house wasn't a surprise to him, knowing Ellen. In the front room the furnishings were old but dusted and polished. In front of the small bay window was a table covered with a cloth of antique lace on which sat a vase of fresh flowers that Ellen had cut this morning in honor of the man who had so lovingly grown them.

"Make yourself at home," she said, self-consciously, knowing he was inspecting her humble surroundings. "I'll make the coffee."

He sat at one of the chairs by the window table because a straight chair was more comfortable for his ribs.

When she came back, Cody was staring out the window, deep in thought. She sat in the chair opposite him and leaned on the table. "The street is more run-down than it was when you left."

"More empty houses." He turned to her. "This is a friendly house. It's welcoming. Gives me a good feeling."

"Thanks. It will be sad to leave it, knowing it will likely go to ruin like the others. No one buys property here."

"Maybe the street could be revived," he mused.

"With its reputation? I doubt it." She met his eyes. "Does it bring back bad memories for you?"

"Some, sure. But there are good memories, as well."

"One thing it does is provide the impetus for kids to leave and find a better life. You've done it. And I will, too." She noticed how straight he was sitting. "Cody, you're just out of the hospital. Are you okay?"

"You keep asking that. Don't I look okay?"

"You look a little tired."

"Haven't slept well. Who can sleep in a hospital?"

"How did you find out about Gramps?"

"I had a premonition when you didn't come back to see me, so I asked around." Cody's voice lowered. "He wanted you to be free, didn't he?"

"Free to leave here, yes."

Cody sighed. "I understand why you want to get away from Pebble Street."

"Every day of my life I've dreamed of leaving." Ellen rose. "The coffee must be ready."

Over several cups of coffee, served in her grandmother's hand-painted china, and chocolate cake sent over by her boss, they talked of familiar things, even the big old lilac bush at the side of the Reillys' garage, which still bloomed every spring.

When Cody leaned on his elbow and rubbed his forehead, Ellen asked, "Does your head hurt?"

"I guess it takes a concussion a while to heal. Do you have any aspirin?"

"Yes, I'll get them."

This time he followed her into the kitchen and accepted the tablets with a glass of water. Cody didn't want to leave her alone, but the pain and fatigue were taking their toll. He knew he couldn't sit up much longer.

She watched him carefully. "You're in pain."

"I'd better get myself home," he said, knowing there was no point in denying the obvious.

She accepted the glass back. "You don't look as if you could make that long walk home. I think you'd better rest."

He protested, "I came here to be your pillar of strength."

Ellen laughed. "If I leaned on you right now, I think you'd fall over."

He was resting against the chipped tiles of the kitchen cabinet. "I hate to admit you're probably right."

"Stay and rest, then. There's a bed upstairs." The door to her grandfather's room was still closed; she hadn't gone in there or touched anything. That left only her bed for him to lie on.

"I've been trying to be tough," he said as he followed her up the stairs, feeling discomfort in each step. "But the truth is, I doubt I could walk all the way back right now. The painkillers have worn off and I'm worn-out."

"Hospitals don't like it when you leave without permission."

"Hell, it's my body, not theirs."

The moment he stepped into the room, he knew it was hers. The white furniture and lace curtains and flowered bedspread were what he'd have expected.

Ellen pulled the bedspread aside. "Lie down and rest. You won't be disturbed here. It's quieter than the hospital."

"Hmm. And far more pleasant." Gratefully, he sat on the edge of the bed, kicked off his shoes and lowered himself onto the pillow. Getting up and down was the worst, except for sneezing or coughing. Once finally comfortable, he said, "You look like you need rest yourself and I've taken your bed. It's a big bed. If you want to lie down, too, there's room."

She stared down at him.

He opened one eye in response to her silence. "Hell, I'm not dangerous. Do I look dangerous?"

"Frankly, no. You're moving like the tin man."

What's dangerous, Ellen thought, *is the way I feel.* The sight of this man lying on her bed was unnerving, almost erotic. It made her realize how cut off she had been from her feelings, from emotions—quite deliberately cut off, to keep something like this from ever happening. Cody had wakened instincts and longings within her that, once wakened, once roused, were taking over her senses. The longing was filling all the empty spaces inside her and tugging at her heartstrings and every vortex of every emotion. With each day of knowing him, gazing at his strong, well-shaped hands, listening to his mesmerizing voice, seeing the depths of his eyes, the longing had become more acute, until now the pent-up emotions were right at the surface, ready to explode.

The grief of the past few days had halted her panic, but ever since she'd felt him take her hand in the cemetery, the hunger and longing had returned full force.

Seeing him lying on her bed was even worse torture. His eyes had closed at once. To all appearances, he was already asleep. It was hard not to lean down and touch him. *Why?* Ellen asked her traitorous heart. *Why him? Why now?*

RAIN CLOUDS HUNG stubbornly over the valley for the rest of the afternoon, gathering strength as the hours passed. By six o'clock a wind had come up and blown in reinforcements.

Cody woke to the sound of rain on the roof. For some moments he didn't remember where he was, until, as the rain pounded harder and a tree branch scraped against the windows, he smelled the soap-scented sheets of Ellen's bed, and then became aware of her warmth.

She was asleep beside him, curled on the far edge of the bed. She had changed from her dark dress to jeans and a loose blue shirt. Her feet were bare. The room was filled with shadows because the sky was so dark. It was impossible to guess what time it was, but he must have slept for hours.

He stretched, testing the pain in his torso—much better. Sleep had helped tremendously; he knew it would.

"Listen," he muttered sleepily. "It's raining hard."

Ellen glanced at the clock on the table. "I can't believe it. Six-fifteen. I slept for over an hour."

"And I slept four hours?"

She sat up, moving to the edge of the bed. "You must be getting hungry."

"Not yet." His hand touched her shoulder. "You didn't go in to work. Certainly they wouldn't have expected you to."

"I had planned to, rather than sit home alone after the burial. But no, I didn't want to, after all, and you were here and it was raining, so I called in. I sorted through Gramps's things until I felt exhausted and came up to lie down."

He urged her to lie beside him again and to rest her head on his shoulder. "It's nice here next to you, listening to the rain. I haven't known anything as nice for a long time."

They lay still, lulled by the rainstorm. His hand caressed her shoulder. "Ellen, why have you chosen to be lonely?"

The question took her by surprise. "I've explained why I've chosen to be alone, not wanting commitments, but I'm not lonely." It was a lie. Even yesterday she wouldn't have been aware of the lie, but now she was. And it frightened her.

He didn't argue, but he knew. He said, "I've known for a long time that there was something back here for me, even though I didn't leave with any intention of returning."

Not me! she thought, even while allowing herself the luxury of his touch.

Cody leaned closer, so close she could smell his sweet male fragrance. He turned toward her and his lips brushed her forehead, then her cheek, then her mouth. She drew in her breath but did not pull away.

The lips she felt were not the lips of a stranger. It was as if she had known his touch always. His kiss, becoming hot, becoming fire-edged, lingered—gentle and burning at the same time. It was a kiss like no other—filled with the promise of blindingly bright horizons and splendorous paths still unexplored. It left her breathless.

He pulled away only with reluctance, whispering, "You're the most exciting woman I've ever known. I've wanted you most of my life, I know that now. My memories of you pulled me back to Shadow Valley."

"You didn't remember me," she argued weakly.

"I did. Just not consciously."

Teasingly, he blew his breath against her eyes and her lips, cupped her chin in his hand and lifted her face toward his. This time his kiss came deeper. Her heart responded with racing beats, her body with a wave of weakness that wouldn't go away, even when he stopped.

His hand moved over her breast. She felt the warmth and her heart pumping against the gentle pressure. He listened with his hand. "Your heart can't lie, Ellen. You want me as much as I want you."

His touch was like ice and fire together. No sensations were ever like this. "I don't understand what's happening."

"Ah, my sweet, I do. I can feel the trembling in your body. Don't fight your feelings. They're good. They are about love."

Ellen moaned softly, "Oh, Cody... I hardly... I hardly know you...."

He smiled gently. "Take time to get to know me, then. I don't want to rush you." His fingers brushed slowly through her hair. "It's just that being here so close to you in your bed... And the rain... I like rain...."

"So do I," she said.

"Then enjoy it. Enjoy me. Get to know me all you want. You can take the tape off if you like."

Her nerves hummed as he persisted with the seductive invitation. "Why... would I want to take off your bandages?"

"Just to know every part of the body I'm offering to you... to do with it what you will."

Ellen flushed. "And that's... knowing you?"

"It's a very good start, my sweet."

"The tape is there to help your ribs heal and it would hurt to take it off. You shouldn't suggest such a crazy thing."

He smiled lazily. "It doesn't hurt if I lie still. I'm not used to being bound up like this and I hate it. My skin itches. At the hospital they gave me rubdowns—"

"Aha, so that's it."

"No, hey, I hadn't planned to say that."

"But you wouldn't turn down the offer, I'll bet."

"I'd be crazy to."

Ellen sat up. "If it really would make you feel better."

Cody began unbuttoning his shirt. "I'd rather be pampering you, pretty lady, but under the circumstances..."

After all, he had been hurt to save her, Ellen reminded herself. It was the least she could do. She went to the bathroom for her body cream. Cody sat up so she could undo the tape. It was self-adhering tape so he could be rewrapped later. Ellen rubbed the cream on his back, careful not to push too hard. Then he carefully lay down flat so she could do his chest.

Her hands were hot against his cool skin. "You have an angel's touch," he said.

An angel was the last thing Ellen felt like at the moment. The trembling in her body wouldn't stop, and she knew it wouldn't as long as Cody was lying half-naked on her bed and she was touching him. He had said he wasn't dangerous, said it half jokingly because his ribs were sore. But there was a delicious danger about him. She could feel herself being led into some enchanted world where his will would become hers. It was both frightening and irresistible because he was both frightening and irresistible.

"Is that better?" she asked, setting aside the jar of skin cream.

"It is if it makes you feel more comfortable with me." He reached up to her and gently pulled her toward him, to kiss her again.

There was caring in his kiss. Caring more than lust.

As if he read her mind, he muttered, "I'm sensitive to what you've been through this week, Ellen, and my idea of distracting you didn't include . . . this. I won't pretend I don't want you. I want you more than I've ever wanted anything in my life. But I respect you enough not to push myself on you—now or ever."

His deep voice, still a little husky from the long sleep, reached all the way inside her and activated every cell in her body. For the first time in her life, Ellen was being touched by her own loneliness—the loneliness that Cody sensed. And

on the shuddering wings of that realization came the awareness of need. Her need to be wanted, to be loved. And this
man—this incredible, beautiful man—cared for her. Wanted
her. Wanted *her*.

Even more confounding were the helpless sensations of her
own wanting, in return. Just to look at him—to hear his
voice, to find herself in the gaze of his eyes—did things to her
mind and her body that were impossible to fight, however
hard she had tried. The past two weeks had been so difficult,
trying to fight herself. Cody had said he wanted to be her
strength, but he had to know that he was also her weakness.

To feel like a woman for the first time—was it a weakness?
No . . . it was the way life meant for her to feel.

The rain, which had let up for a while, began to beat hard
again against the roof and the windowpanes. Ellen touched
Cody's hard, bare chest and smiled down at him. "You won't
be able to go anywhere in this storm."

He lay his hand over hers, on his chest. "Is that all right
with you?"

Ellen nodded slowly. *Dreams were only premonitions*, she
thought. *But storms brought them together.*

9

ELLEN ASKED, "Do you want the tape on? Would it be more comfortable?"

Slowly moving his body sideways, Cody grunted, "It's not so bad." He sat up, then rose carefully. "I'll test it out on my way to your bathroom. The coffee has gone through me."

"The coffee was hours ago. I'm thirsty and hungry and I know you are. I'm going to get us some supper."

A few minutes later, while she stood in the kitchen preparing bacon and eggs, Cody appeared in the doorway. His shirt was unbuttoned and he was barefoot. *This is like a movie*, she thought giddily. He could be a film hero expertly fitted out and posed to look as sexy as possible. On Cody it was natural; he was a study in male beauty.

"Can I help?" he asked.

Ellen motioned toward the opposite cabinet. "I think I have a bottle of wine in there. Do you want to check?"

He found the bottle and asked for a corkscrew. He poured out two glasses of Burgundy and handed one to her. "To the storm," he said.

"To this storm. Not the one that hurt you." Hating to be reminded of the picture of him lying in the street, she turned to the bacon in the skillet. "I hope you like bacon and eggs."

"Just the right thing for a rainy night. I'll make toast."

Cody found candles and set them on the kitchen table along with plates and flatware. Ellen moved about as if in a dream, because these domestic moments with Cody were so strange and yet so comfortable.

Talking was easy, as if they had known each other forever. Talk of books they had read, music they liked, memories of long-ago days. Forty minutes later they were still at the table. The candles were burning down, and the radio was on.

Cody said, "I like this song. Will you dance with me?"

She looked surprised. "Dance? I've...never danced." This fact had secretly bothered Ellen; there was a plan in the back of her mind to take dance lessons someday, in the city.

Cody didn't express his surprise aloud, if it was surprise. He had been learning how isolated Ellen had kept herself. The more time he spent with her, the more he understood her and her feelings of alienation from the mainstream of life. He offered her his hand and a gentle smile. "There's nothing to it."

She hesitated.

"Just follow me," he said, urging her to her feet and into his arms. "I normally wouldn't be moving as stiffly as this . . . but just get into the rhythm of the music with me."

His arms were tight and warm around her. Her heart beat against his chest. "Isn't there some step I need to learn?"

"Naw, not for this kind of dancing. There . . . That's right. You just feel the music and my movements."

"I'm afraid you'll hurt your ribs."

"Honey, I wouldn't do it if it hurt."

Ellen wasn't sure she believed this, but she would take his word. Before two songs had finished, she wondered why she had never tried dancing. There were so many things she hadn't tried.

"It's still raining," Cody said.

"Buster is going to wonder where you are."

"He doesn't like getting wet. He'll be home, warm and dry."

"Did you really come straight from the hospital to the cemetery?"

He nodded. "They're probably looking for me. I suppose I should have left a note."

She raised her hand to her mouth in mild shock. "When were they going to discharge you?"

"I don't know. It doesn't matter now."

"But are you okay?"

He smiled mischievously. "Maybe I should go to bed. Do you want to lie down with me?"

"I did that once."

"Hmm. And you were starting to get to know me with your magic hands. There is more of me to know."

Butterflies flew acrobatic drills around her stomach in response to such a suggestion. The wine had melted the last of her inhibitions. By now she wanted desperately to know more of him—more of the incredible mystery of him.

Upstairs in her bedroom, Cody stripped down to his shorts and lay down on her bed.

"Nothing very modest about you," Ellen teased nervously.

"Hey, not true! I normally sleep nude."

She flushed. "I don't."

"I figured you didn't." He patted the mattress. "Get comfortable and come sit beside me."

Ellen took off her shoes, nothing more. Cody reached over and touched her hair. "You smell so sweet, Ellen. Your perfume makes me think of fresh flowers."

"It *is* flowers you smell. I don't wear perfume."

He sniffed at her neck. "Flowers?"

"I hate cheap cologne and I can't afford expensive perfume, so I crush flowers with a drop of oil and rub them on my skin."

The expression of admiration that came into his eyes caused her to look away self-consciously.

"You're the most incredible woman I've ever known. The most beautiful, the most creative and the most caring. And by far the classiest. No wonder I've fallen in love with you."

He urged her close until their lips touched, and he kissed her more deeply than before, his fingers lightly caressing her throat.

Her emotions soared out of control. His words were the most beautiful Ellen had ever heard, and the most dreaded. Tears sprang to her eyes. Her plea was raspy: "Oh, Cody, please don't love me. . . ."

He was silent as he lifted her hand and began caressing each finger gently. Looking at her hand, he said, "Why? Because you can't love me?"

"That's not why. You know why. I told you."

"Yeah. But I can't turn my feelings off like a faucet."

"It's all so . . ."

"Overpowering?"

She nodded. *How did he know so well what she was feeling?*

"It's overpowering for me, too, Ellen. I don't know why meeting you has put me in a tailspin. I could say it was because I had dreamed about you when I was a kid, but I was spiraling before I became aware of that. I must have remembered subconsciously who you were."

"I must have subconsciously remembered you, too," Ellen muttered. "It's the only explanation I can think of." *Other than Meredith's explanation involving the lure of the ghost, which I don't want to think about.* Meredith hadn't let her forget. She had insisted that tomorrow, when Jeff was out of town, they would break into the mansion and see if they could find a . . . solution to this mystery. Tomorrow, though, was a long way off. Tonight could last forever as far as she was concerned. . . .

"Explanation for what?" he was asking.

"For you popping up in my dreams."

"Speaking of dreams . . ." Cody began, and quickly forgot what he had been about to say. Conversation didn't interest him at the moment; he began kissing her fingers lightly, one by one. "Ellen, no woman has ever looked at me the way you do. I know you want me. Maybe as much as I want you."

Her heart was racing again and the butterflies were back.

His fingers, like licks of fire, moved up her arm to her shoulder, slid under the collar of her shirt and caressed her bare shoulder, then descended to her breast, touching the lace. He bent down and kissed her breasts, over her shirt.

"You're tense when I touch you," he murmured. "I don't want you to be tense."

What do you expect? she wanted to scream. Ellen couldn't trust her voice not to crack under pressure of the overwhelming sensations assailing her body and her mind. And her heart. She wanted this to stop. And she wanted it never to stop—not until she knew every secret there was to know.

"Don't be afraid to touch me," Cody whispered, urging her hand to his chest. "Feel my heart beating? It's exactly in sync with yours." With the other hand over her breast, he said, "See? Same rhythm."

"That's incredible." Her self-consciousness began to ebb. "My heart doesn't usually beat this hard."

He smiled. "Neither does mine. And my body doesn't usually tingle all over like it's doing now. Or get as heated up..." He coaxed her hand down along his solar plexus to his waist. "I still have the feeling you're more comfortable getting to know me first. Here...don't be afraid to touch me...."

"Cody..." she began, and her voice faded into the sound of splashing rain against the windows. Her hands *did* want to know him; and with him, all the mysteries....

He closed his eyes. "Hmm...the hands of an angel." He wriggled out of his shorts and lay luxuriating in the sensations, feather light but more sensual than anything he had ever known. Feather light—and somewhat timid. Even as he began to take note of her timidity, his soaring passion overrode logic.

He reached out to release the buttons of her shirt, and slid it off over her shoulders. Ellen, wildly aroused, wanted to be closer and closer still, to lose herself completely in the spell of consuming passion that engulfed her. *How could it be like this? As strong as this?*

Unzipping her jeans, she pulled out of them and drew herself against his body, whispering his name, welcoming the gentle explorations of his large, experienced hands.

"Honey," he said, "you're trembling all over."

"I can't help it. I think it's passion."

He frowned, and asked carefully, "Think? Don't you know?"

"Well, not . . . not for sure. I feel . . . I feel so alive, so full of energy and so helpless at the same time. It's hard to describe. It's what you do to me. . . ."

Cody swallowed. Earlier he had been thinking that because of his cracked rib and the problem of exercising his back too much, Ellen would need to take the initiative—eventually. God, he'd been more than blind! He'd been an idiot!

He bent to kiss her, ignoring the discomfort of the position. He kissed her gently, savoring the taste of her and the faint scent of flowers, and the pure, magnificent essence of her innocence. She returned the kiss, her arms folding strongly around him, her breaths coming in fast waves over her heartbeats.

"Honey. . ." Cody whispered. "I'm rushing you. It isn't fair to do that. You're trembling as if you're afraid."

Her voice was weak and jagged. "Not of you . . ." She paused for what he thought would be forever, then said, "Cody, I should tell you—"

His heart constricted with sensations of pure love. "It isn't necessary to tell me." He kissed her eyelids softly, then her temples and her cheeks and her lips.

Ellen felt herself being guided down in the bed, felt him reaching for the sheet, which he pulled over them, and then she was wrapped in his arms, feeling his body relax alongside hers.

"Just let me hold you," he said. "Just wrap my love around you and hold you. That's better, my darling. Just know I'm here with you and allow the trembling to go away...."

Her words were muffled against his strong shoulder. "Cody...?"

"I didn't mean to rush you," he repeated. "I didn't realize but I should have. You said you'd never danced. I should have realized then. Lie beside me awhile and know I love you, Ellen. Cuddling is one of the best things there is. Isn't it?"

"It's wonderful," she said, nestling closer.

"Cuddling on a rainy night."

"Hmm..."

"Waking in each other's arms."

Tears formed in Ellen's eyes. She was glad he couldn't see them, but he probably knew they were there. His sensitivity overwhelmed her. It *was* uncertainty that had caused her to tremble. Self-consciousness. Cody was so worldly, and she existed in self-imposed exile from life as others knew it. There were questions she had been afraid to ask in the whirlwind of emotions he'd swept her into. He was putting her feelings before his own.

With Cody's body warm and solid beside her, Ellen had never felt so protected or so happy. *So this is what love is. And the rest? The ultimate ecstasy? Tomorrow?*

Cody unfastened her bra under the blanket, slid it away and cupped his hand gently against her breast. "Tomorrow..." he murmured, as if he had read her mind.

Ellen closed her eyes and fell into the rhythm of his breathing. From her body came little shivers of desire that could not be quelled. *Thank you, Cody,* her heart said. *Thank you for understanding....*

IN CODY'S DREAM, *he and Ellen were dancing in a grand blue ballroom under sparkling chandeliers. She was in a gown of ice-blue silk that flowed and fluttered as she moved in his arms to music he couldn't hear. Light made her jewels sparkle, but brighter jewels shone in her eyes, which looked up into his and smiled. And her lips smiled as if saying,* I belong here ... in this room ... in your arms ...

There were no other people in the room. Cody could smell the flowerlike fragrance of her hair. He leaned down and whispered, "Where are we, Ellen?"

Her voice was like the sweetest music. "Don't you know? Don't you remember?"

"Tell me."

She laughed. "We're in the mansion. The ghost is watching us, but I don't care. We don't care, do we?"

IN HER DREAM SHE WORE *ice-blue silk chiffon trimmed with pearls, and a diamond necklace at her throat, and satin slippers. Dancing in Cody's arms was like dancing on clouds; one could dance like this forever and never tire. She easily recognized the blue ballroom of the Whitfield mansion. Above them were the crystal chandeliers, and somewhere near lurked the ghost who always watched. Cody seemed unaware of the figure. She gazed up into his eyes, which tonight were bluer than her gown, and he smiled because they were together...dancing...touching. He whispered,* "Where are we, Ellen?" *as if he didn't know.*

AT THE FIRST LIGHT of morning, Cody woke to find her still beside him in the bed. It hadn't been a dream, his being here. The dream was about that mansion again. For a second time since the storm his dreams had come unblocked and he could remember. His attentions quickly turned to the beauty of the morning—the scent of Ellen's body and her hair, the sunshine filtering through the lace curtains at the window of her pink-and-white bedroom. He kissed her cheek, aware that the movement wasn't painful. She stirred. Her eyelids fluttered open.

A sleepy smile formed on her lips. "Hi."

"Hi," he answered.

"Umm, you're really here, Cody. You're not a dream."

"Definitely not a dream."

"It isn't raining anymore," she mumbled. "The sun is shining. I must open the window and let the morning in."

The smell of rain-washed earth blew in as Ellen, wearing only lace panties, took an enormous breath before darting into the bathroom. When she returned he was sitting naked on the edge of the bed.

At the sight of him, the butterflies flew in her stomach again and the promises of yesterday returned as fresh as the mountain morning air. As Cody left for the bathroom she stepped out of her panties.

When he came back, Ellen, propped up with pillows and thrilled at the sight of his body, gazed at him unashamedly. Smiling, she held out her arms. "Come back to bed."

His smile met hers. "An invitation I can't take lightly.

"How beautiful you are," he said as his hands moved across her bare shoulders and down over her breasts. His lips followed the path of his fingers in a trail of fire. Ellen sucked in her breath, trying to take in the sensations. Her trembling fingers teased his thick dark hair and then lost hold as he moved lower, raining kisses over her whole body.

Only after a time did she become aware how stiffly he had to move. "Cody... your back..."

"Who can think about my back?"

"I can. Please... lie down flat."

He did as she asked without a word. He didn't have to be reminded of the pain, even as lost as he was in the magic of Ellen's beauty.

On his back, he looked up into her misty eyes. She smiled down at him, her fingers spread out over his chest, moving sensually over his stomach, his waist, his abdomen. "I don't know what you've done to my heart, Cody. You've made me want you so."

He smiled dreamily. "I didn't sleep much last night, with my body telling me how near you were. And now, you here, touching me... I don't think I can control my reflexes too much longer. I'm only a human male...."

"You definitely are."

He groaned softly at her touch, luxuriating in the wonder of her, submersing himself in her acceptance of him—the most beautiful adventure of his life. Being with her was where he belonged. Finding her was like finding the lost part of himself.

He looked into her eyes—sensitive blue eyes glistening like dewdrops catching the light of the summer sun—and in those moments he knew more about love than he ever imagined. He said gently, "You're not protected, are you, honey?"

"Oh. Oh, no." She shook her head. "My whole body is spinning, Cody. I feel like Alice falling down the hole into Wonderland. Or was it Dorothy... or a naive kid named Ellen...?" She wasn't making much sense; how could she, when her tingling, spiraling body was controlling her head?

He smiled so lovingly it seemed unnecessary for her to try to figure out what it was that she was trying to say.

"Not naive. Nor innocent. You are a woman who knows and respects herself. Waiting for what's right. The wonderland is love . . . and I'm falling down into it with you . . . and I wish there was nothing we had to protect ourselves from. Since I wasn't planning this, I don't have anything, either. But it's okay. There are other ways."

She gazed at him for a time, feeling her pulse throbbing in her throat and spiraling down, awakening every female cell of her body. The energy of her own pulse was exploding in her. "Then guide me."

"Is that what you . . . what you want, Ellen?"

"Guide me," she repeated on an exhaling breath, moving both hands over him. "You implied that there is magic in my hands. . . ."

He moaned with pleasure. "Ah, my love, there is!"

"Then show me," Ellen whispered. "Show me how to believe in magic."

He moved his hand over hers. "You're the one leading me right now, to a place of no return. You already know, my love."

How was it possible to feel such weakness and such power at the same time? Ellen wondered, realizing her intuitive touch was rendering him quite helpless.

"You're making me crazy," he muttered. His quick breaths filled the silence of the room until they were more moans than breaths. "I can't—" he began, and the word caught on a shudder of release. His eyes closed. He trembled.

Ellen, caught in a whirlpool of passion, kissed his closed eyes. He looked at her dreamily. "My sweet love . . ." Reaching up, he caressed her hair and her face with his fingertips. "I want you to feel what I do."

His fingertips moved to her breasts and along her body. Gently he urged her onto her back and leaned over her, raining kisses upon her—kisses that felt like butterflies dancing. Her whole being floated and fluttered with them.

His hands began to explore again, gently, then more boldly, searching for her weakness and her power and her feminine beauty. Searching. Finding. Possessing. She moaned with pleasure.

He whispered, "Just let it be, Ellen. Just let it happen. . . ."

As if she could do anything else. She closed her eyes and invited in the seduction of his passionate hands and the luxury of his love.

Until stars burst behind her closed eyes.

She felt herself falling into a pool of light made by the fragments of the stars.

10

DREAMS, CODY THOUGHT, were warnings. Years ago he had
been warned of the falling tree branch in a dream, and because of the dream, long forgotten, he had saved Ellen from
serious harm. Now his dreams had returned. Twice he had
dreamed of himself and Ellen in the old Whitfield mansion.

Warning glimpses of danger.

Ellen, too, had dreamed of that place. What it meant, Cody
couldn't fathom. He only knew something in the old house
was a threat to her. Its ghost, perhaps. She had spoken lightly
of ghosts, without fear. But forewarnings came in strange
disguises; this he knew from the outcome of his early dream.

Danger lurked behind those walls.

While Buster trotted off down the path tracking the scent
of a squirrel, Cody stood at the rusting gate, looking up at
the mansion. It stood reclusive and aloof against a gray-blue
sky, a sad, forsaken old outcast, confined to silence, clinging
to its noble dignity. Unwanted, ill-omened, friendly it was
not.

Strangely, it looked as distant as when he had seen it as a
child. Like the other kids of Shadow Valley, he had always
pedaled by quickly, never looking up. In those days the gate
was chained shut.

The chain was still there, its lock holding tight, but the
hinges of the iron gate had long since corroded away. Only a
leaning post held the gate vertical. Cody touched the bars
with some hesitation. He didn't belong here. Yet his dreams
indicated otherwise. Something was in that deserted house

that he needed to know, and it had to do with Ellen. With Ellen's safety.

The gate creaked and groaned in protest as he pulled it against a barrier of tall, thick-stemmed weeds. Buster, not wanting to be left out, followed, but when Cody started up the weed-grown path to the door, the dog whined a protest.

"You don't like this place, huh?" It was not a good sign, because normally Buster was curious. Tail down, he gave his friend an I'm-not-going-up-there look and scooted off sideways, rounding the hill, picking up another interesting scent.

"What kind of sport are you?" Cody called after him. "Not afraid of ghosts, are you?"

He proceeded up the hill alone until he moved into the invisible shadow of the house, where, whether he imagined it or not, the air felt cooler. He kept climbing until he reached the narrow, railed porch. His dreams had hinted of elaborate ceremony. One ought to be highborn and well fitted-out to enter such a grand estate; jeans and boots seemed almost disrespectful.

"Hell, I'm not intimidated by you anymore," he said aloud to the imposing structure. "Maybe you've had impressive beginnings, but now you've known privation, same as me."

He made his way up the steps. The door was locked; he knew it would be, even though in his dreams it had been open to him. There were still curtains at the windows, shielding the inside from the eyes of intruders like him.

As Cody circled to the rear of the house, Buster was nowhere to be seen. The back door was also bolted. With each passing moment he became more certain that the house didn't want him there, and more determined to get in. If there was a threat here, he was going to find it now, not wait a dozen years as he had done after the last warning dream.

He checked the basement windows one by one until he found one hidden by iris stalks and twining morning glories that had a torn screen and broken pane. With his knife, Cody was able to jimmy the lock and pull open the window. Dust rained on his head as he lowered himself down into the bowels of the house.

In the dim light, he pushed aside cobwebs and hurried toward the stairway that led to the kitchen. Cody knew exactly where he wanted to go—the dining room where he had seen Ellen. And a ghost. His footsteps echoed on the wood floors of the hall.

At first he didn't recognize the dining room, now bare of furnishings, until he saw the chandelier. Covered with dust and cobwebs, it hadn't caught sun rays for many years. Heavy curtains darkened the room. Cody looked around, astounded. No question, this was where he had been in the dream. Those were the same maroon drapes over a series of narrow windows. The same fireplace framed by elaborate carved woodwork. He moved to the place where Ellen had turned to greet him. Here she had taken his hand. *How could he have known what this room looked like?*

As in his dream, Cody had the feeling he was not alone. Tensing, he listened but heard nothing. His eyes, adjusting to darkness, scanned the corners of the room. A shadow darted across at the edge of his vision.

A shiver began at the back of his neck and coursed down his spine. The ghost was really here!

"Who are you?" he asked softly. And he thought, *Why were you invading my dreams?*

Against a far wall was a tiny shadow quivering like the flame of a candle—a candle Cody couldn't see. As he stared at it, strangely he had the same sensations as if he were staring into an actual flame. Mesmerized, he began to hear soft strains of music. His head went light and he felt himself becoming dizzy. He blinked repeatedly to make the vertigo go away, but when he closed his eyes it was worse.

Then the room suddenly came to life. The shadow of the flame flickered from a silver candelabra on a table set with flowers and gleaming china. Voices surrounded him, and then faces came into view.

A dinner party was in progress. The women wore dresses trimmed in beads. Each one had upswept hair held with sparkling combs. The men were in dark jackets. The talk was congenial, happy, but a sense of something being terribly wrong swept over Cody.

At the head of the table sat a woman with light hair and an oval face like Ellen's. The likeness was distinct—the small sensual mouth and wide blue eyes. She was holding a wine goblet and smiling at a gentleman seated next to her. But the smile was not genuine. Her eyes were tormented, frightened—not of the man, who must be a guest; she was frightened of something hidden and sinister. Was the woman Ellen? She looked different, but surely it *was* her. This time he wasn't asleep. He was under the spell of a very haunted house.

The vision faded in seconds but the vertigo remained. Cody leaned against a wall holding his head, wondering what was going on. What had he seen? A party that had taken place in this room decades ago? Or was it in his own imagination? Hell, he didn't have that good an imagination! No question about it, the house was not only haunted, it was bewitched. And somehow it was connected with Ellen.

And so was he, in his dreams.

The room darkened with late-afternoon shadows. Thick cobwebs on the chandelier quivered; the curtains moved slightly as if someone were passing by. The silence was oppressive.

Ill at ease, with the vision of the party and the woman stubbornly clinging, Cody was eager to get out of the decaying mansion. He turned his back on the dining room and what he had "seen" there and walked into the foyer, from which opened two front parlors, one on either side of the house, each with a bay window. These rooms had been beautiful, once. He glanced up the staircase with no desire to climb it only to find more dust and cobwebs and echoes of the past.

Normally, he would be rushing up to satisfy his curiosity, but something else was going on. The strange energies of the house were pushing him away. Yet at the same time, they were pulling him in, because of their connection with Ellen, whatever the hell that connection was.

And his own bond with Ellen? More real than dream? To his annoyance, it seemed impossible in the setting of his dreams to know the difference. Tracing his steps back through the kitchen and the dark basement, Cody couldn't get the flash imagery of the dinner party to leave—not simply because the woman resembled Ellen, but because of the fear he saw in her eyes.

DURING THE NOON HOUR of that same day, Ellen waited for Meredith at the side of a rain-rutted back road that led to the Whitfield mansion. She was apprehensive over Meredith's idea of going inside, but she'd always ached to know what it was like.

Meredith pedaled up on a three-speed bicycle and dismounted, catching her breath. "I'm not late, am I?"

"No. I was early. I'm not sure about this, Mere. Breaking and entering—"

"To tell you the truth, I'm not sure about it, either, now. Not after your grandfather's funeral. I was so astounded to see Cody there."

"So was I. I thought he'd be in the hospital a few more days. He turned up out of nowhere. What'd you think of him?"

"He's a hunk, all right. Too much so. A woman can get caught in the snare of a guy who looks like that." They had started to walk, but Meredith, pushing her bike over the bumpy, hilly road, dawdled. Her usual vivacious enthusiasm definitely wasn't part of her persona today.

"Is something the matter?" Ellen asked.

"Yes. We have to talk. When I saw how Cody was at the cemetery, holding your hand so protectively, not caring *who* saw him . . . I mean, at such a time—" Meredith stopped still. "Well, I have to tell you, Ellen, I got some very strange vibes."

"What kind of vibes?"

Meredith turned to look at her childhood friend with concern in her eyes. "I felt danger."

"Danger?" Rarely did Meredith's psychic pronouncements surprise Ellen, but this one did. *Danger* was a strong word.

"Something has happened between you two," she said. "I sense something odd going on. When I was thinking about you this morning, trying to get some kind of psychic message, the pattern of tea leaves in my cup gave me quite a start." She looked into Ellen's eyes. "Thank heaven I remembered to warn you about the consequences of kissing Cody while he was unconscious."

"Why bring that up?" Ellen asked apprehensively.

"The leaves. They warned of . . . of separation."

"Separation is a given. We already know that. I can't see what it would have to do with danger." Ellen sighed. "Anyhow, Meredith, I'm not as superstitious as you."

"Superstitious? Is that what you call my psychic insights? After all this time? All these years? I thought you were a believer."

Ellen felt a slight chill in the summer breeze that ambled down the side of the high mountains. "I am, to a point. But there are some things. I mean, where do you get some of this stuff, like kissing a sleeping man causing bad luck?"

"From Mrs. Volken, of course. There isn't anything she doesn't know. And I've never known her to be wrong. The ancient ways of her people . . ." Meredith's voice slowed to a stop. She turned to Ellen again with anguish. "Omigod, Ellen! Tell me I'm not reading between the lines, here! Surely you can't be saying that you didn't heed my warning?"

"I didn't heed your warning, Mere."

She raised her hand in horror. "You're kidding me, right?"

"Hey, I couldn't help myself. He looked so . . . beautiful lying there and I was feeling a lot of gratitude because he got badly hurt saving me. If it hadn't been for Cody—"

"You kissed him?" Meredith interrupted, her mouth still agape. "When he was unaware of it?" She shook her head. "That means you set bonds with him too soon. It means . . ." She paused, scratching her forehead. "It means there will be an intense physical relationship followed by heartbreak because of uniting too soon." Meredith held her hands, crossed, in front of her. "No. It mustn't happen. Maybe there is some way to reverse—"

"It's too late for reverse," Ellen said softly.

Meredith's eyes rounded as if she'd seen a snake crawl by. "What? The two of you? But no!" She lost her grip on the handlebars of her bike and it toppled over with a thin crash. Letting it lie there, she plopped down on a grassy embankment with a howl. "You vowed you would leave Shadow Valley . . . without ever . . . !"

Ellen sat down on the slope beside her. "Don't you think you're overreacting?"

"It's because of that kiss in the hospital."

The two women sat in silence for a time. Laughter of children sounded from down the narrow lane, and soon they caught sight of two boys and a dog running across the road. Ellen remembered how as a child she often came by this very spot on her way to see the mansion. Now, after all this time, to be headed back there again, but with a bizarre plan to break in with her old partner in crime . . .

"It's because I can't help loving him," Ellen countered. Silence ensued, broken only by the distant barking of a dog. "I don't want to but I do," she muttered weakly.

Meredith shook her head in wonder. "I've often secretly wished you'd fall in love with a local guy and not leave home, not leave me. Though, of course, I've always understood why you have to."

"Even falling in love can't stop me from leaving."

Silence fell over the pair of friends, until Ellen broke it. "Are we going to sit here all day getting our seats grass-stained? I thought we had a mission to accomplish."

Meredith was thoughtfully chewing on a weed. "The mansion, you mean. We can't do it now, Ellen. We absolutely don't dare."

"Why not?"

"Believe me, you don't want to take that risk. It's too dangerous. It's because you connected somehow with this guy in a dream state, and then you sealed the passion when you kissed him when *he* was not in waking consciousness. And you have fallen in love just weeks before you want to find another life. To go into the mansion now would bring horrendously bad luck."

"I'm not following you," Ellen said.

"Mrs. Volken has talked a lot about the dangers involved in making a transition from waking to dreams. She says spirits of the dead can communicate with us in our sleep. Something like that must have happened with your dreams. That ghost is in there, Ellen, and maybe it is what's interfering in your dreams. You don't dare get close to it. No telling what it could do."

"That's pure speculation," Ellen replied, not wanting to admit that Meredith's words were giving her chills. There had never been a reason to fear the ghost of Whitfield. On the other hand, she had always believed the gypsy woman of Pebble Street knew matters of the occult; it would be foolish to defy her warnings.

"Ask Mrs. Volken about ghosts and dreams," Meredith advised.

Ellen sighed. "No. Mrs. Volken gives me the creeps. You've always known that. To tell you the truth, I wasn't too keen on breaking into the mansion, anyhow. We probably couldn't have gotten in." She rose from the bank and pulled the bicycle by its handlebars to an upright position.

Meredith got to her feet, stretched, and brushed clinging seeds from the seat of her jeans. "May I remind you of what I've always said—the reason Mrs. Volken disturbs you is because deep inside, you know the truth of a gypsy's powers. She says I have gypsy blood and that's why she's been willing to teach me so much."

"Damn it, Meredith, you've paid her to teach you."

"Even so, she won't work with just anyone." Meredith held her hand out defensively. "Oh, don't say it."

Ellen smiled. "I know you're psychic. I've seen your predictions come true too many times not to know it. I respect your opinions, even though sometimes I really don't want to believe, in bad luck and such. I want to believe we make our own luck in this life."

"I believe that, too, to a point," Meredith said. "But there's another dimension around us where spirits are supposed to live and not interfere with what's going on in our dimension. Yet too many of them think they have unfinished business on our plane, and since they've lived here, they sometimes hang around instead of going to wherever it is spirits are supposed to go after their earth life is over. They interfere with people. Some even cling to people. I had one clinging to me once.

Mrs. Volken was able to communicate with it and demand that it leave."

They were walking back down the gravel road toward town, Ellen pushing the bike. Ellen was tiring of the subject of ghosts. Her mind kept wandering back to Cody and the sensation of his warm breath against her neck. She thought, too, of Meredith's remark about the curse of separation. What difference did it make if she'd kissed Cody when he was asleep? They were destined to separate anyway. If she hadn't kissed him, would she have been able to resist making love to him? Had her kiss somehow reached some depth of his being and caused him to get up out of his hospital bed and come to her, wanting her?

Or had Meredith been taken in by an old gypsy woman who made things up?

Chances were, if she had heeded Meredith's original warning, she would not be suffering the pangs already—the awful pangs of having to leave someone she loved.

11

IT WAS ONE OF THE MOST important days of her life, a day for celebrating. So why did she feel so sad? Ellen closed her portfolio, carefully tying a red ribbon around the large folder. After all this time, all these hours of saving and working and planning, her last assignment was finished. Underneath her pride of achievement coiled a sick and nagging loneliness.

She sat at her bedroom window, gazing out at a lazy summer midmorning on Pebble Street, feeling the warmth of the sun on her arms. Two barefoot children were playing with a dog at the end of the street. A cat scrambled through the high, weed-grown grass along the curb and ran into an unpainted shell of a garage. It was like a thousand other summer days of her life, and yet it was like no other.

The house was so deathly quiet. Below were the flowers of her grandfather's garden, now carefully tended by Ellen. She sighed. For years she had worked for this day...this reward...this ticket out of Shadow Valley. Now victory was as empty as the house.

Leaving meant leaving Cody, too. If only he would go with her, but with each day that passed, he became more a part of the town's very foundation. He was carving a place for himself with innovative ideas for promoting the radio station and Shadow Valley with it. He was here to stay. And she *couldn't* stay.

How many plans she had made at this very window! The view of the street of her childhood would be etched indelibly in her mind. The street was inhabited by a thousand ghosts.

The whole town was a haunt of ghosts, as far as she was concerned—ghosts of memories best forgotten.

She turned, hugging the precious portfolio to her chest, and laid it on the bed where she and Cody had slept together and where she had fallen in love. Love—the mind-altering condition she had tried so hard to avoid.

It was so tempting to share with Cody the news that her assignments were finished and there were only the final exams to complete, which were easy for her. What would he do if she told him? Take her out to celebrate? Hardly, knowing what it meant. No, this was one celebration she couldn't share.

AT SIX O'CLOCK IN THE evening Ellen met Cody at the radio station, from where it was only a three-block walk to the hotel. People still stopped Cody on the street to inquire about his recovery. Those same people were becoming accustomed to seeing Ellen at his side, but the staring never ceased, because the Ellen Montrose they now whispered about looked as if she had just stepped from the pages of a high-fashion magazine *and* she had snagged the town's handsome newcomer. These were against the rules Shadow Valley lived by. Pebble Street white trash were supposed to know their place. She felt the stares as she and Cody walked in the mild summer breeze.

He took her hand. "You look stunning, as always."

She smiled a thank-you. "I never imagined I would ever wear my design clothes in Shadow Valley."

He glanced sideways at a passing couple. "I'm proud of you." He had been well aware of the stares, even when Ellen wasn't dressed up. The town had noticed he stopped by the café to walk home with her after work. That was when invitations designed to set him up with certain town socialites had intensified. Being a child of Pebble Street, he knew they were trying to stop him from seeing Ellen. Not just because of who she was, but because of who they thought *he* was—the best catch in town. He chuckled at the thought.

Ellen said, "I worry that your association with me will hurt the reputation you're building. People don't understand why you mingle with the likes of me."

"Ellen, don't be ridiculous!"

"It's true and you know it. It's why you haven't let them know where you're really from."

He frowned, slowing almost to a stop. "At first I thought they might remember me, but they didn't, with my different name. I haven't tried to hide it, and when the time is right I fully intend to reveal where I was born—when the impact will be the most effective. But that's not the subject. What we're talking about is you and me together. Don't you know, Ellen? I'm proud of the woman I love and I'd shout it to the world!"

"Why?" she asked, genuinely puzzled.

They had reached the steps of the hotel. Two older women leaving the building gazed curiously at the young couple, she in a chic white pleated dress with tan trim, he in brown slacks and tan sports jacket. Cody smiled and held the door for the women.

When they were seated at the table, with the wine list, he asked, "What do you mean, *Why?*"

It took a few seconds for Ellen to remember their conversation. She paused. "I mean, why would you be proud?"

He blurted out, "I'm with the most elegant woman in town! They see that and can't deal with it."

This brought a breathless smile to her lips. "Am I really?"

He reached across the table for her hand. "Are you kidding? You have a mirror. You can see your reflection—and I see the effect of it everywhere you go."

She watched the waiter pour their wine, then raised her glass to meet Cody's. After a long pause, she said, "Thank you for the compliments. I'm an end product of a lot of hard work."

"Class is born," he said. "You might have added a finishing touch or two to make up for early circumstances beyond your control—and I don't mind telling you I'm in awe of your talents. You've studied hard, perfected your speech, created beautiful clothes, but you didn't create your mystique. You *are* it." Uninvited, his vision of a dinner party in the Whitfield mansion assaulted his mind . . . and the frightened eyes of an elegant woman who looked so much like Ellen. They were not Ellen's eyes. With profound uneasiness, he forced away the eerie picture, hating mysteries he couldn't understand.

When she held the stemmed glass, Ellen noticed her own hand trembling. Her ego wasn't used to such extravagant strokes. This man who sat across from her with the candle-light shining in his blue eyes—there could never be another man like him; never, in all the earth. There could never be another voice like his or a smile like his or a love like the love he offered her. . . .

But what could she give him? A wife who had been a waitress at a truck stop? That's what she was and would always be in Shadow Valley. It was all so useless. To break this chain of frustrated thoughts, she set her napkin on the table. "Would you excuse me while I find the ladies' room?"

The women's lounge was mirror-lined and papered in pink-and-silver stripes and bathed in pink light. Ellen was seated on a velvet-cushioned chair powdering her nose when a woman sat down beside her. The reflection in the mirror was smiling, and familiar—Doreen Engleson, wife of Shadow Valley's mayor.

Ellen returned her smile. Who would ever have dreamed she would be sitting beside Mrs. Engleson in an elegant ladies' room?

"Your outfit is stunning," the mayor's wife said.

"Thank you." Ellen continued to powder her nose.

"Truly stunning. I saw you here before in a black polka-dot outfit that people have been talking about ever since." Doreen Engleson looked both ways to make sure no one else was in the room before she leaned in closer, turning from the mirror to meet Ellen's eyes. "You must shop in Denver. Would it be rude of me to ask what boutiques you've found?"

"I don't shop in Denver," Ellen replied.

"Really? Where, then? Oh, my dear, how indelicate of me to ask but I'm just dying to know." The diamonds on her fingers sparkled when she extended a hand. "We haven't met, but I know you are Ellen Montrose. I am Doreen Engleson."

To her surprise, Ellen liked the woman. She saw no disdain whatever in her eyes, only unbridled curiosity. She accepted the jeweled hand and said simply, "I made the dress I'm wearing."

Doreen reeled. "What? But how is that possible?"

"It's my own design, Mrs. Engleson. I'm a designer."

The woman's hand flew to her throat. "Ellen! You *designed* these magnificent outfits? My dear, I am a *very* fashion-conscious individual and I recognize high style when I see it. And on you I see it! You're not having me on, are you? You truly *did* create this?"

"From scratch."

"But *how?*"

Ellen smiled. "I told you. I'm a designer, a graduate of Galleau School of Design, which originated in Paris, with studios in New York." It was the first time she had said it aloud.

This seemed too much for the mayor's wife. Her eyes glazed and she began to sputter, "But you . . . you work. . . ." The sentence floated in the air between them.

"Yes, I work at the truck stop," Ellen finished. "It's how I paid for my school."

"Amazing! Utterly amazing. Such talent right under our very noses. And no one knows." She glanced toward the door. Her voice lowered to a whisper. "Ellen, would you make a dress for me? The fall festival grand ball is coming up next October and I have been beside myself trying to find the right thing to wear. Oh, would you? It would be our secret. I'll pay you three hundred dollars, not counting the fabric."

Ellen didn't know whether she should feel honored or insulted. Inside warnings leapt up to remind her she tended to be too sensitive. Luckily, the few swallows of wine had relaxed her, and Doreen's manner, up to now, did not offend. By her own admission, Mrs. Engleson knew high fashion but it didn't sound like it, to hear her now.

Thoughtfully, she responded, "I'm afraid it's out of the question. I'll be leaving soon for New York."

The woman seemed almost desperate. "Oh, please, Ellen, it would mean so much to me. When are you leaving? The affair is still some months away. I could make it five hundred."

This was a lot of money for one dress, and for Ellen. New York was expensive and there was no guarantee of how soon she could find work. It was tempting. But it was hard to shake off the niggling feeling of being exploited. The autumn ball was the big social event of the year in the county, with every socialite trying to outshine every other.

Ellen smiled. She heard a voice that sounded like her own talking as if from a distance and then growing stronger. "We're not talking about a dress, but a gown. My designer gowns start at a thousand dollars, not including fabric. I must choose the material myself because it is an integral part of the design." *Take it if you recognize a bargain,* she thought. *Or leave it if you don't.*

Doreen Engleson's eyes were sparkling in the over-the-mirror lights. Her voice was soft. "For a custom-designed gown, that's reasonable. Yes, fine. Do we have a deal, then?"

Ellen nodded, trying to keep from revealing her momentous excitement. *A thousand dollars!* It was true, her designs *could* compete with those worth that and more. But she wouldn't have dreamed of *this!*

"Could we keep this a secret?" Doreen asked. "I want to surprise everyone." A wicked giggle turned into laughter. "I want to knock them dead is what I mean, of course." She fumbled with her white leather clutch bag. "Now, my dear, I really don't know where you've been hiding, and I can't risk your changing your mind. I'll give you five hundred now and five hundred on delivery, plus, of course, the cost of the material—if that's satisfactory."

Ellen tried to keep her voice even. She had never held a check for that much money in her life. "We'll need to do two fittings. I'll do them at your home."

Mrs. Engleson didn't look up from her diligent check-writing. "Excellent. I appreciate that."

Ellen rose, inspecting her hair in the mirror.

The woman handed her the check. "Remarkable," she muttered, shaking her head. "Your designs are remarkable. And you wear them like a trained model."

"I have trained," Ellen said, smiling softly. *A hundred nights in front of my mirror with a book on my head. Ten thousand strides across my bedroom floor and down the stairs. A thousand pirouettes for graceful turning. Copying heroines in movies. Oh yes, I've trained.* Nonchalantly, as if it were something she had done many times, Ellen slid the check into her elegant envelope handbag—a purse made from a yard-sale hand-embroidered heavy lace tablecloth that she had offered twenty-five cents for because it was "too stained to use."

"Can we meet tomorrow?" Mrs. Engleson asked. "Could you stop by midmorning and we'll discuss gowns over a cup of tea?"

"I could come by around ten." *A guest for tea at the mayor's house. This business of being a graduate designer was everything she had imagined—even more.*

A part of Ellen wondered how Doreen Engleson secretly felt about inviting a Pebble Street resident to her home. It was a first in Shadow Valley, certainly. Well, it was a service kind of thing, after all. The tea was just for politeness. She had something Mrs. Engleson wanted. The fun part was how far the woman was prepared to go to get it.

Cody rose when she returned to the table, just the way she had seen well-bred men do in Hollywood films. *He, too, has observed and practiced,* she thought. *He knew about wine and social graces and he had learned proper speech, too. Well, of course, the speech—he was a radio announcer.* Her admiration showed in her smile. It was odd that she hadn't realized until this moment how very much alike they were. Cody had been as determined to shed the stigma of his past as she.

"Why the funny look?" he asked.

She leaned in close, whispering, "I've just made a thousand dollars, Cody! A thousand dollars! Mrs. Engleson asked me to make a gown for her."

His eyes widened in amazement. "One dress? A thousand dollars?"

She suppressed a giggle. "I can't believe I had the nerve to ask that. But I knew if she wanted a high-style gown made especially for her, she couldn't do it anywhere else for that. I also saw how much the mayor's wife wants to outdo everybody else. She jumped at the opportunity." Ellen's hand rose suddenly to her mouth. "Oh, dear! I promised Mrs. Engleson this would be a secret and already I've broken my promise. You mustn't tell anyone, Cody."

"A secret?"

"Yes. And I take pride in being a woman of my word. Promise me you won't mention this to anyone."

"I'm amazed." He grinned. "So that's what took you so long in the ladies' room."

"An interesting place, the ladies' room. Where else would I find myself elbow-to-elbow with the town's first lady? She said very complimentary things about my clothes."

He raised his wineglass. "Here's to your talent, Ellen. To your many talents."

His eyes were beguiling, hinting of passion they had known and passion they had not yet even explored. She flushed, finding herself getting lost in the magic of his aura and feeling the butterflies again.

"You didn't promise," she said weakly.

"What?"

"Not to tell."

"Oh, that. Yeah, sure."

Her smile was seductive; she knew it and couldn't change it. "We'll drink to your talents, too, Cody. I'm beginning to think we are two splendid people."

"Superb people." Opening the menu, he glanced up with mischief in his eyes. "Now. Let's see if the chef has come up with any appetizer worthy of our exotic tastes."

THE FOLLOWING AFTERNOON Ellen was in her room filling out an order form for fabric from a prestigious firm in Chicago when a messenger came to the door. The boy presented a note from Mrs. Skyler, wife of the town's senior doctor, asking to meet with her about designing a gown.

How could this have happened? Mrs. Engleson surely wouldn't tell; the doctor's wife was one of her fashion rivals. And no one else knew except Cody.

Could there have been an eavesdropper somewhere at the restaurant? The waiter? It hardly seemed possible because she had been very careful about keeping her voice down. Who, then? How?

News of Mrs. Engleson's gown had spread across the social set of Shadow Valley in a matter of hours. By evening there was a third request—a telephone call to the café from the wife of the owner of Harlow's Hardware, Inc.

The mayor's wife was going to have a fit. Ellen would have to reassure Mrs. Engleson that she hadn't betrayed her trust and promise to guard the personal design of the dress with her life.

Nevertheless, worry over the gossip leak was assuaged by the thrill of what was happening. Three thousand dollars in less than twenty-four hours! Before she checked out that night, Ellen gave notice at the café, promising to work part-time until a replacement was hired. Her boss was not surprised; he had always known that when her grandfather died, Ellen would not stay in Shadow Valley.

Cody was attending a town meeting that night and couldn't meet her after work. It was just as well, because Ellen had things to do. Working until far past midnight, she moved some bedroom furniture downstairs to make room upstairs for another cutting table. It was a wonderful opportunity to make money before leaving, even though she had money saved. The house was up for sale, but no one was likely to buy it. She would sell what furnishings she could and abandon the rest. The dresses she had already contracted for would take several weeks, especially with having to work on such an old machine. This was a delay her original plans had not called for.

Was it really the money? Or was it the chance to work as an honest-to-God professional designer whose talents were sought after? Or was her eagerness to have this work an excuse to be a little longer with Cody?

"WHY DON'T YOU STAY?" he asked, when she told him about the calls and the orders. "Stay and go into business here."

"Here?" She just looked at him sadly.

They were sitting in swings in the park, drinking lemonade purchased from a stand at the entrance.

"Yeah, here. Obviously you have something everybody wants."

"Not as an ongoing thing, Cody. There aren't enough women here who would pay such high prices for their clothes on a continuing basis. Right now there's a big competition. The interest will peter out."

"I'm not so sure."

"Anyway, I could never live here, for all the reasons you know very well."

Cody had taken off his shoes and socks to feel the cool of the grass, a carryover habit from his childhood. He kicked at the dust under the swing. "You and I have different approaches to life, Ellen. My idea is to attack and conquer. Yours is to escape."

She bristled. "That's easy for you to say. You left when you were seventeen. I've had to stay and pretend to my grandfather that I adjusted to what I couldn't adjust to in a lifetime. You made good and came back. I can't fathom *why* you came back, but you came back a different person than the kid who left."

He was twisting the swing sideways; the chains were grinding together over his head—a noise that bothered Ellen, but Cody didn't seem to notice. "I thought you knew why I came back. There were two reasons, one that I just told you—to conquer the past. To be accurate, I ran off like you're running off but that was different, too. All I had to my name was a guitar. You are now in demand. People have recognized your talent."

"How did it happen?" she asked.

"What do you mean, how? People saw you dressed in outfits they'd die for. That's how."

"They didn't know I had designed them. Now they do. And the only people I told were Mrs. Engleson and you. It was supposed to be confidential and in no time it was all over town."

"What about your friend Meredith Calhoun? Didn't she know?"

"No. I might have sworn Meredith to secrecy but I didn't even have a chance to tell her. Meredith probably wants to kill me for not telling her before she heard it on the village drums. Good thing I don't have a phone." She shook her head. "It's just such a mystery. You didn't tell anyone, did you?"

"Me? Come on, Ellen."

"Well, someone did."

"Shadow Valley is a haunted town, you know. Unexplained things happen."

She pulled a face. "Well, there is an explanation, somewhere. I thought Mrs. Engleson would be furious but she wasn't, which is odd, as if she might know something I don't. Maybe she's the one. Though I really can't believe that."

"Hell, why worry about it? It's a lucky thing. Gives you more reason not to rush out of my life."

A light summer breeze fanned her hair and her pink summer skirt as Ellen's swing moved slowly back and forth. Her hands perspired on the chains. It was hell talking about leaving. All her excitement had turned into pain. In one way she resented Cody for the pain. He hadn't given up any dreams to be with her. Why should he expect that her dreams were any less important? Cody of all people should understand why she could never become what she wanted to in this place. The subject should have been closed from the day they met.

"You said there were two reasons you came back," she reminded softly. "But you only told me one."

"The other is obvious. To find you."

It was like a piercing of her heart. "Oh, Cody. Don't."

"It's the truth. As far as I'm concerned, I've loved you since I was a kid and dreamed about you. I don't believe in coincidences. I was drawn back because you were here. That's why I loved you almost from the time you first sat across from me in the Silver Nugget with the candlelight shining in your eyes. I knew I loved you, but I didn't tell myself so in actual words. In the storm, seeing you in the streetlight. I consciously knew it then. I remembered you."

"What you're saying is...impossible." Ellen had gone weak, as though all the blood were draining out of her body and taking her strength with it. He was referring to one dream—one long-ago dream. What would he do if he knew the whole truth—that she had dreamed of him, too, the night before they met?

Did those dreams really mean that the two of them were meant to be together? No, because "they" couldn't be! Sitting together in the summer sun, Ellen wasn't able to bring herself to look at him for fear the pain in her heart was showing in her eyes. It wasn't fair that a bunch of crazy night dreams could twist and cripple the joys of her future dreams. It wasn't fair that she loved Cody and leaving him would be like a part of her dying. It just wasn't fair!

12

HE KNEW A BACK WAY in to Pebble Street. The old alley was overgrown with brush, except for a footpath still used by local kids. It circled behind the houses on the east side of the street, one of which belonged to Mrs. Volken.

He was fairly sure the kids still crossed themselves when they passed that particular house. Why would that change? Nothing else had. The same rails were missing from the small back porch. The same faded blue curtains hung at the windows. The same wooden planter with one scraggly geranium sat by the door, and not a spot of paint had touched the building anywhere.

How old must the gypsy woman be by now? He'd thought she was old twenty years ago. Some people, it seemed, grew too old to die, and it was said that gypsies were not ordinary people.

Ellen would be home working on the dresses, and he didn't want to take the chance of her seeing him. Making his way under the leafy trees at the side of the house, he stepped quickly to the front door, knocked loudly, and waited for a full minute before the handle turned and the door squeaked open.

The gypsy had not changed. In fact, Cody could have sworn she was wearing the same rust-colored skirt and dark-flowered blouse he remembered. Gold chains dangled from her neck. Her dark skin was wrinkled but her dark eyes were clear and ageless.

She smiled as if she had been expecting him. "Kevin Reilly. Well, well, a surprise. When a lad leaves Pebble Street, he seldom returns."

He smiled. "I'm the exception then, Mrs. Volken. I'm glad to see you're still here."

She motioned him in. "As long as there are people who need me, I'll be here. What can I do for you, lad?"

"I need some information and advice."

"Of course." She led the way to a small room decorated with travel posters of France and Greece and furnished with a table and two chairs. On the larger chair, which had once been green, stretched a fringed, flowered shawl. Cody waited until Mrs. Volken had settled in comfortably before he sat down in the opposite chair. Except for the posters, it was amazingly like what he'd imagined a fortune-teller's "office" would be. A yellow cat appeared from nowhere and leapt onto her lap.

Mrs. Volken gave him a businesslike smile. "You are concerned about your future with a particular woman, are you not?"

He nodded. "It's complicated. I need to know something about dreams, Mrs. Volken. And about ghosts."

Her face suddenly became solemn, her eyes darkened. She closed them and turned eerily still, sitting with one hand resting on the cat. With the other she reached toward him. "Give me something of yours to hold."

Cody removed a tigereye ring that had belonged to his father and set it in her hand. He sat back and waited.

"You are very tense," the gypsy said. "Find the rhythm of my breaths and breathe with me. Deeply. Try to relax. That's better. I will give you my impressions. Then, if you have specific questions, I will try to answer."

Her eyes remained closed. "This woman. Although you have met her very recently, you have known her before. There is something murky in her family background which even she might not know. She lives here in our valley of shadows. She loves you but she will leave you. You are here because you want to stop her from leaving."

Cody's mouth had gone dry. He had always believed in psychics, but her insight amazed him. "Yes," he muttered.

"You have had troubling dreams about her. Something is unusual about your dreams.... I can't quite get what it is...."

"There was a ghost in the dreams," he said. "An actual ghost, not something out of my imagination."

Her fingers tightened on the ring. "Ghosts in dreams are usually not a good thing, lad, because spirits of the dead can influence our thoughts through dreams. This spirit is female, I sense that. And you have seen her."

"Only hints of her. In the Whitfield mansion."

Mrs. Volken's head lowered, as if she had gone deeper into trance. "The discarnate being is trying to lure someone into her domain.... Not you... A woman. I think it is the woman you love."

He drew a shaky breath. "Why?"

"I don't know. Some spirits willingly communicate with me. This one will not. But I sense pain and suffering in that house. It is not a good place to be. I believe the ghost is using dreams to lure her. I can almost get the name.... Iris? Ellen?"

"Ellen," he said.

"The woman who intends to leave you."

"Not me. Shadow Valley. And I intend to stop her, any way I can."

The old woman nodded. "Ah. So now we get to the real reason you came."

"Right. You say this ghost can manipulate dreams. I thought so. I know for a fact Ellen has dreamed about the mansion." His eyes fixed on the gleam of gold of her necklaces in the light from a small bulb directly overhead. This news was not good. If he were to tell Ellen the truth—that the Whitfield ghost had a fixation for her—she'd find it all the more reason to distance herself from the town. He said, "I want to know how dreams are manipulated so I can do the same. Nothing else has worked to convince her."

The gypsy opened her eyes for the first time since she sat down. "Do you think I know the secrets of the dream-world?"

"I hoped you might. A lot of people talk about your knowledge of magic. And it's common knowledge that you can contact the dead."

"The latter is true, lad. Many spirits want the opportunity to speak through me. Some don't. They control the communication, not me. And yes, I can often read fortunes when the energies are properly aligned. But the dreamworld is full of mystery. I am a seer, Kevin. I'm not a witch."

His spirits were getting heavier by the moment. "So you're saying it can't be done?"

"No. It probably can be done. I am saying that I don't know how to do it. I strongly recommend that you not pursue this idea, dear. Interference in the dreamworld can open us to dangers beyond imagining."

Cody sat back. "Danger to Ellen, too?"

"If a ghost is involved in her dreamworld, it would become very angry and make a lot more trouble than it's doing now."

Rage rose in him. "Curse it, Mrs. Volken! There has to be something I can do. If I can convince her not to leave, then there will be time to deal with this ghost thing. Right now, I just need to persuade her to stay with me. What persuasions do you know?"

"Such persuasions come under the category of witchcraft, my dear Kevin. I'm afraid you would have to find a witch for that kind of help."

"Come on," he coaxed. "There has to be something."

"I can take a better look into the future, this is where my power lies. The outcome of future events can be changed, to be sure. But only you can do that—you and she."

He frowned, discouraged, but unwilling to give up. "Take a better look into the future, then."

Mrs. Volken closed her eyes and concentrated, her face losing all expression. "You have a distinguished future in Shadow Valley. I see you in some kind of public office. And there is something to do with communication, perhaps radio—"

"Never mind all that stuff," he interrupted. "What about Ellen. Will she leave?"

"Yes, there is no question about it. She will leave."

Cody felt his heart sink. "No. I'll stop her."

"I don't think so." The gypsy handed back his ring and looked at him with wise, dark eyes. She said, "I'm afraid I haven't helped, except perhaps to warn you to be careful about the dreams."

"Which is a good thing, I'm sure." He rose and reached into his pocket and lay some bills on a dusty side table next to a set of Tarot cards. Interesting, he thought, that she had used psychometry with his ring and not cards to read his future. The stuffiness of the house, combined with odors of cooking, was getting to him and he wanted out.

"Blessings to you," the woman said, patting back strands of gray hair.

"And to you, Mrs. Volken. I'll be back one day."

As she was walking him to the door, a knock sounded. To his surprise, it was Meredith Calhoun who stood on the old woman's doorstep, and the familiarity between the two was evident. Meredith and the gypsy... very curious. Meredith stared at him. "Cody Laird? What a surprise finding *you* here!"

He smiled. "Life is full of surprises." *Including Ellen's surprise as soon as Meredith told her about seeing him here. He'd need a good explanation. Unless he could get to Meredith before she had a chance to talk to Ellen.*

He found her later at home when he knew her husband was at his clinic.

"Is there no end to the surprises?" she said when she opened her door.

"I want to talk to you."

"About Ellen, I'll bet." She motioned him into her living room. "You're not smiling, Cody."

"Neither are you. I think you know I'm here because I saw you at Mrs. Volken's."

"I've been very curious about that. But Mrs. V. wouldn't give me a clue."

"Does Ellen ever talk to the gypsy?"

"No. Not that she's a disbeliever. She has me around if she wants psychic advice." Meredith smiled for the first time. "And even if she doesn't, she still gets my advice."

"She doesn't go for Tarot readings or anything like that?"

Seated across the coffee table from him, Meredith kept strong eye contact. He saw that she was suspicious, but he didn't care.

"Why don't you ask *her*? Meredith said.

He sat back. "Because I'm up to no good. You already know that, so why should we beat around the bush? What is your relationship with Mrs. Volken?"

Meredith's lips tightened; her voice became stiff. "I suppose you could say I'm her student."

Ah, he thought. *This is even better.* "Does that mean you know something about Tarot?"

"I read Tarot cards." She cocked her head. "Why?"

"The cards carry powerful messages. If they came out a certain way, most people would hesitate to go against their predictions."

Her eyes narrowed. "Are you asking me to do a reading for Ellen?"

"I was thinking about Mrs. Volken, but you'd be even better. You know what I'm getting at, Meredith. I want you to manage the reading so it'll come out with a strong warning that she shouldn't leave."

Meredith's hand flew to her throat. "That's horrible! What sort of person are you?"

"A desperate one." He met her eyes. "I'll do anything to stall her long enough to convince her where she belongs."

Anger showed on Meredith's face. "Oh, really? You think she belongs in a town that has been so unkind to her?"

"She belongs with me. Shadow Valley can be conquered."

"Just what would you know about it? You're a stranger." Meredith folded and unfolded her hands nervously. "Ellen believes you care for her. Why would you want to trick her?"

"I don't want to trick her. I want to marry her."

Her body froze in shock. "Marry? You want to *marry*—"

His eyes fixed on hers. "Will you help me?"

"Oh, Lord." Meredith rose and began to pace. "I want more than anything for Ellen to stay. She's the sister I never had. I'll be devastated without her."

"I hoped that was the case, knowing what your friendship means to her."

"But it's her life dream, Cody! Something she has to do to find her identity. She's planned it her whole life."

He watched her pacing. "Ellen doesn't have a valid picture of how harsh the world is or how competitive, in spite of her impressive talent. She's chasing rainbows."

Meredith sighed. "I'm afraid of that, too. She's so . . . sheltered. But she's also a strong, determined woman. It would take a lot to stop her."

"I intend to stop her."

"With my help?"

"With or without your help."

She scowled, but her voice was soft. "It's selfish."

"A man's love is like that when a thing is meant to be."

Meredith continued pacing. "I need a drink. Want one?"

"Sure."

She disappeared and returned with two glasses of whiskey. "So you want me to manipulate a Tarot reading, to jeopardize my integrity, lie to her. She took a long drink. "All right, I'll do it." Another drink steadied her voice.

"I'll be forever in your debt," he said.

Meredith set down her glass and looked him in the eye. "If you ever let her know, I'll kill you."

"I'll always respect your friendship," he promised.

She held his gaze. "As much as I want Ellen to be here for my sake, that's not why I'm agreeing to this shameful conspiracy. It's because I believe in love. I'm convinced you love her. And she is in love with you."

"THIS IS A FUN IDEA," Ellen said, handing up a jug of lemonade to Meredith from the top of the tree-house ladder. "You were right, I do need a couple of hours off. I've been practically sewing in my sleep, and it's been ages since we came up here in the daytime." With the high trees shading them, it was the most private place in town, and a spot where they could be kids again.

When they were settled on the floor with ice clinking in their glasses, Meredith said, "I brought my Tarot cards. I think we should do a reading for you."

Ellen smiled. "Great. It's been years since you've done a reading. Now's the perfect time, almost at the crossroads."

Meredith handed her the deck. "Here. Shuffle and cut and think of the question you want answered."

"The question is, how will my life change when I leave? What will happen with my career?"

"Okay. I'm going to do a Celtic-cross spread, which means you turn over the ten top cards. Go ahead with the first."

Ellen turned a card faceup. "Six of Cups."

"This describes the situation. It represents creating new atmosphere, meeting with an old friend. That must be me."

No, it must be Cody, Ellen thought, and said nothing. She drew a second card.

"The Sun. Oh, dear, it's reversed. That means uncertainty, loneliness, depression from loss of a relationship."

Ellen felt uneasy. "Swell. Maybe we shouldn't do this, Mere."

"Hey, it can get better. This isn't the entire story. Here, see? The next card is the Lovers. A man and woman bonded in love. This placement is hope and aspiration."

Ellen sat numbly as Meredith continued, turning card after card. Nine of Pentacles, reversed: poor judgment. Eight of Swords: trapped by insecurity and fear. Ten of Cups, reversed: lack of fulfillment. Queen of Swords: a strong, unyielding woman; barrenness, separation.

Meredith seemed to be getting nervous, as jittery as Ellen. "I'll admit this doesn't look very good as far as your decision to leave," she said. "This is . . . weird." She looked up. "But we have to keep going because the last three cards are the most crucial and could be more hopeful."

Ellen sighed and reached for the eighth card. "The Fool? Oh, terrific. What does *this* one mean?"

"It's your attitude in the matter. It portrays an imaginative mind but a misinterpretation of the environment."

"What? A misinterpretation of my environment? You've got to be kidding."

"Cards don't kid. They merely inform. The next one will be significant. It will reveal your hopes and fears."

When Meredith caught a glimpse of the ninth card, she sucked in her breath. The picture was a burning tower in a raging storm with a full moon shining. "The Tower! Damn!"

"It means disaster, doesn't it?" Ellen wheezed.

Meredith's voice became very soft. "It represents a disruption, or failure, but failure that can lead to a new life."

"Are all the cards so horrible?"

"No, but yours happen to be less than encouraging."

"The last card has to be better than the Tower."

"The last card gives the outcome of your question."

Ellen sighed heavily. "I guess we might as well look."

Below nine swords, a woman covered her face in despair as she leaned over what might be a casket. Ellen stared at it in horror, then looked up at Meredith. "Well?"

"I have to be truthful," her friend said hesitantly. "This card represents disappointment, loss of self-assurance, and disturbing dreams. It's not a positive message."

"So what should I take all this to mean? In relation to my question?"

"It's pretty clear, isn't it? What happens will be disappointing, not what you expect. In fact, Ellen, the cards are warning you not to go to New York."

"But that's ridiculous." Even as she said it, Ellen felt a surge of fear. Meredith had turned almost white. Yet she must have had misgivings beforehand or she wouldn't have suggested consulting the cards.

"It's not ridiculous and you know it. You need to think about this."

Ellen was near tears. "It's not as if I had choices."

"There are always choices." Meredith touched the Fool card. "This one is damned interesting. Misinterpreting your environment."

"Only a fool could do *that*."

"I dunno, buddy. I'd like to be positive but this is upsetting. How long will the three gowns take to finish?"

"Two to three weeks, at my present rate. I work long hours. I've turned down offers to create two more."

"You won't leave town before I get back. Jeff and I are leaving for two weeks in Seattle. He has some kind of horse seminar and I'm going along. Have you had any time to see Cody?"

"Some, but I resist it. The more I see him, the more I'll miss him. It's just . . . too hard."

"He can't be very happy about that."

"No. He works long hours himself and has all sorts of projects, but he'll always make time for me. I'm the one who's being difficult. I'm not equipped to handle all these new emotions."

"Your life has suddenly become pretty complicated. And I'm not helping, am I? With this Tarot reading. Damn it, why don't you stick around here awhile longer, see what develops with Cody?"

"After knowing me all my life you're suggesting—?"

"I go by the cards," Meredith said. "The cards don't lie."

13

IN THE LIGHT FROM A *window high in the mansion stairwell the shadow of a bird fluttered against the wall. Ellen drew back in alarm, filled with unease and not wanting to climb any farther into the mysterious house. Some unseen presence, however, was impelling her to go higher.*

A sound of breathing was so near. The presence horrified her, but she couldn't stop herself from following it. She looked back into the darkness below, thinking she heard a dim echo of footsteps. Where was Cody? Why didn't he appear? He should be here, like before, but he wasn't. She was alone with the ghost.

This didn't feel like the other dreams. The ghost was too close…too real. Frightened, she wanted to call out for Cody, but something stopped her.

She turned and gasped. The filmy figure of a woman floated in the stairwell behind her. The ghost wore veils, white and gauzy and wafting in a breeze that wasn't there. Her face was indistinct. Ellen felt her pulse throb in her throat; her knees trembled. The ghost hovered, making escape down the stairs impossible; there was no way to go but up.

She reached the topmost landing from which a pillared archway led into the ballroom where she and Cody had danced in another dream. Opposite the arch was a small open door revealing a stairway to the attic. The ghost drifted toward the ballroom entry. It was as if Ellen were being herded like a sheep to slaughter, but as dismayed as she was, a cu-

*rious excitement was pushing her. Something was up there.
Something important.*

*The stairway was dark and steep and extremely narrow.
Halfway up, Ellen thought she heard Cody call from somewhere below in the depths of the house. Immensely relieved,
she called back. Her voice echoed against the confining walls.
Turning, she wanted to race down to find him, but the ghost
was behind her. Light illuminated the eerie white form although there was no source of light in the stairwell. What did
the ghost want? Why did it keep moving upward, blocking
her way down? "There's no place left but the attic!" Ellen
breathed, in a vain attempt to argue with the phantom.*

She called Cody's name again before she rushed the remaining distance up, because the figure was getting so close
she could feel a chill and smell an odor of sweet perfume. The
stairwell was closing in like a cage!

A low-ceilinged attic opened up before her. Light flowed
in dusty streams from a high window. Old furniture and
trunks and boxes were stored here amid dust and cobwebs.

Suddenly the ghost was in front of her, moving through the
shadows toward a far corner where it hovered and shivered,
as if caught in a chill wind. The sight was so macabre, Ellen
shuddered. Did it want to be followed now? To that far, dark
corner? No, I can't, *she thought. This was the ghost's abode,
and Ellen had no intention of remaining in it. Now was her
chance to bolt back down the stairs. With eyes still fixed on
the apparition, she backed up slowly and turned to run. But
a shadow filled the doorway.*

Cody!

Thank heaven!

His voice came like a sweet, deep echo. "Ellen! What is it?
What's wrong? Are you all right?"

She tried to run to him and couldn't. Her feet wouldn't move. Her voice caught in her throat with a choke. "Cody! Do you see it?"

Brushing aside cobwebs, he took a step forward, into a beam of light where disturbed dust sparkles were dancing. In that light was also the brightness of his eyes turning from blue to silver. His gaze was fixed on the far corner and the ghost. What was he seeing there?

Abruptly, Ellen awoke. She looked around in the darkened room, confused. What had wakened her she didn't know. The only sounds were those of night crickets. She had wakened too soon; the dream was incomplete. What had Cody seen?

She sat up stiffly, trying to shake off all the images and sensations of the dream, but they wouldn't leave. She leaned back against the headboard and stared at the dark ceiling. *It was the same ghost she had seen in the window when she was a kid!* That same filmy thing floating behind the upper windows.

The ghost's will had been compelling her to go to the attic. In the dream, Ellen had been unable to go against that will. Frustrated, she threw aside the blanket, found her robe and headed down to the kitchen. Cody had wanted to come by last night after he got off at the radio station, but she had insisted she had to work late on the gowns. If he had been here, would she have dreamed of the ghost?

Why not? He had been lying beside her when she dreamed they were dancing in the blue ballroom. Overcome with a new emptiness, Ellen began to pace, wanting something desperately, not knowing what. She picked up an apple from a bowl on the counter, washed it under the tap, and then slammed it into the sink in a frustrated burst of anger. *Damn it! Why the mansion? Why always the mansion? What was it about that empty house that haunted her—literally haunted her? Why wouldn't it leave her alone?*

The ghost—was it real? Had she *really* seen it those many years ago? "This is too much!" she said aloud. "This has gone on long enough! I want to find out what this is all about! Somehow I've got to get into that house, whether Meredith thinks it's bad luck or not!"

JUST LIKE IN THE PAST—so often in the past—Ellen found herself in front of her own haunted house gazing up at the small windows under the roof. The ghost's attic. It would be dark in the house, but as long as it was daytime, some light would shine in through the high windows. If she was going up there, it had to be while there was still daylight.

There had to be a way.

Anticipation of the unknown stiffened her whole body as Ellen made her way up the front steps and tried the door. As expected, it was locked. Looking to make sure no one was around, she circled the house and tested the back door; it, too, was locked. She walked along the side, brushing aside weeds in old flower beds, feeling strange to be so near the house at last.

A basement window would be the only way. Stepping cautiously to make sure she wouldn't scare up a snake, Ellen found a broken window. The grass was pressed as if someone had been here recently. Kids, maybe. After three hard tugs, the window opened far enough to crawl through!

She let herself down into the depths of the big house and looked around intrepidly. Wires lined the space under the ceiling, strung for drying clothes; otherwise there wasn't much here other than a wooden table, two iron lawn chairs, a wheelbarrow, and a wall of closed cupboards.

She hurried up the stairs to the kitchen, a small room with white-painted cabinets, and rushed from there to a center hall.

Standing there in the front foyer, gazing into the living room, Ellen gasped in surprise. The house was still partly furnished. Yet it looked nothing like it did in her dreams. Although the layout was amazingly the same, the furniture was plain, bordering on shabby. In her childhood imagination, it had been so magnificent, with beautifully carved antiques and splendorous fixtures. And in the dreams it had been the same.

Her disappointment was unreasonable, Ellen scolded herself. After all, who would leave priceless furnishings here to gather dust, year after year? This was just old stuff that wouldn't be worth trying to sell piece by piece, stuff Carolyn Meullar had no use for. It was not like in her dreams. Yet how did she know the layout of the house when she had never been here?

Ellen walked from room to room in fascination. Behind the shabbiness of the furniture and the layers of dust was a solemn, imposing beauty. Stately pride. It was as wondrous as she had imagined, because she could see beyond the neglect to the possibilities. Something was vaguely welcoming, and something was more than a little frightening. The ghost . . . was it here?

It *was* here! Ellen knew she wasn't alone. She could run back to the basement window and get away, but the energy of the house—or of something in it—held her captive. She had come because she had to know what her dream meant; and she was going to find out, no matter what. This left no choice but to go to the attic.

The oak-railed staircase with its high window sending down shafts of light was exactly like in her dream. The window reminded her that if she wasted any more time, evening would bring darkness.

Her footsteps made no sound on the worn carpet of the stairway as she forced herself to begin the climb. She reached the landing where Cody had appeared in her first dream. The mysterious echoes of the house were unnerving. Her own breathing was too loud. By the time Ellen reached the third floor, her hands were ice cold and her heart was thumping. Glancing behind again and again, she half expected to see the ghost appear as it had last night, but the stairway was empty.

Still, she *felt* it. There *was* something or someone here, and the feeling was strongest on the third floor. Propelled by the ghost's energy, Ellen turned left at the landing and found the door to the attic stairs. Not wanting to linger on the narrow stairway, she ran to the top. . . .

The attic looked exactly as she had "seen" it, and this was astounding. How could she have known? Ellen stepped into the shadowy room. She turned slowly toward the corner. The ghost was there—hovering as before! Ellen drew a startled breath, but the apparition was not as frightening as it might have been, had she not expected it. Like in her dream, it floated in filmy white veils. A woman? Ellen's fear eased; the ghost wasn't threatening, after all.

Trembling, she took a step forward, and the ghost moved slightly away as if it didn't want to discourage her from approaching the mysterious corner. It *had* led her here.

She sensed movement in the doorway behind her. Ellen's heart jumped. What if someone found her trespassing? She turned around.

"Cody!"

"Ellen?"

"What on earth . . . are you doing here?"

As stunned as she, he had not moved from the entry. "Here in the attic? I might ask you the same—" His voice stopped abruptly. His face registered astonishment. "The ghost!"

Staring at the filmy spirit, he said incredulously, "I dreamed this!"

Ellen reeled with dizzy disbelief. "*What* did you say?"

He brushed aside cobwebs and strode into the empty space between them. To her astonishment, he addressed the ghost directly, as he had done before, when he couldn't see it. "Who are you?"

The apparition merely stared.

Ellen touched his arm. "Cody, did you say you dreamed this?"

"Yes, exactly this. We were here—you and I and . . . her."

"Last night?" she asked in a high, weak voice. "You dreamed last night that we were here?"

"Yeah. I thought there was something important in this attic, because the dream was so real. . . . I felt compelled to—" He stopped and moved his eyes from the ghost to her, remembering Mrs. Volken's warning about Ellen coming into this house. "Why are *you* here?"

Her voice broke. "I dreamed it. Last night. The same thing."

"My God!"

Neither of them spoke for a full thirty seconds. In that time the light in the attic brightened as a cloud moved out from over the sun. Ellen fought for composure, wiping at a tear on her cheek. Finally she choked out, "The same dream?"

"In the dream I came in and found you exactly as I did now. And you turned around and said my name, just like now. Was it a dream or a premonition? Or *what*?"

"I don't . . . know! Cody, I don't know! That . . . ghost! It doesn't move. It just stays there, right where it—"

"Where it led you," he finished when her voice halted. "I woke thinking there's some secret here. Did you come through a basement window?"

"Yes . . ."

"When I saw the window was open, I wondered for a split second if you were here, and then forced the idea out of my head." Cody said this as he was inching forward. "Why this corner? There's nothing here!"

She was right behind him. "But there must be. Why else would we both dream it and feel it so strongly? Why else would the ghost linger? Why wouldn't it disappear?"

Looking constantly over their shoulders toward the hovering spirit, they knelt down, and Cody ran his hands along the wall. "Here's a loose board."

Ellen watched while he tested the board to see how much it would move. As it rotated sideways on a single nail, the adjoining board moved also, to reveal something solid behind it. He reached in and felt a handle.

Ellen gasped. "There *is* something hidden! The ghost *did* deliberately lead us to it!" When she turned around, the specter was gone.

"No question about that," he said. With a yank, he pulled out a small, scratched leather suitcase.

She muttered, "She has left . . . I think."

He brushed dust from the case. "Maybe now that we've found what she wanted us to find, she doesn't have to stay."

Ellen rubbed her eyes. "A ghost conveying messages in dreams? Oh, it's too much to . . ." She watched him examine the rusty lock. "What is it? Can you get it open?"

It took some jimmying to get the sides to part. Silence filled in with the dimming light as he pulled it open to reveal the contents: a few papers, a leather-bound notebook, and a box tied with a blue ribbon.

Ellen lifted out the notebook and opened it, moving it to catch the dim light from the window. "It looks like a diary of some kind. There's a date. 'February 17, 1902.' And a name. 'Iris Whitfield.'"

Mrs. Volken's warnings no longer were important to Cody. Ellen was safe as long as he was here. He was supposed to be here, with her. The dream was proof of it. He was searching through the papers, which appeared to be legal documents. The light was too dim to read the fine print. "The writer of the diary must have hidden this case," he said. "Well hidden. For a reason."

"Maybe we'll figure it out when we read what the diary and these papers have to say." Ellen flipped through the pages of the notebook. Each page was handwritten, carefully. Near the back of the diary, the handwriting was more hurried, less precise. She said, "It's too dark to read it."

"Let's take the case downstairs."

Ellen looked over her shoulder to see if the spirit had returned. The attic was quiet, full of only cobwebs and shadows, with no sign of any ghost. She slid the diary back into the case.

Cody said, "The stairway is almost completely dark. Let me walk ahead of you so if you trip you'll fall on me."

"And what if you trip?"

"I won't. I can see fairly well in the dark and my eyes have already adjusted." He headed for the stairs, carrying the case.

Their footsteps on the wood echoed in the narrow stairwell. The house was beginning to feel familiar to Ellen even though it was her first time actually inside. She felt she'd been here many times, and in a mysterious way, she had. With Cody here, all her fear of being inside had vanished.

From the wide landing, they stood looking into the arched entry of the ballroom. There was no furniture. In the ceiling plaster were two holes where chandeliers had been removed. The walls remained a vivid sky blue, against an ornate white molding along the ceiling and white wainscoting on all four sides. Darker patches marked rectangles where oversize paintings had once hung.

"What a room," Cody wheezed.

"I've dreamed of this room," she said softly. "I dreamed that you and I were dancing here. And in the dream the room was blue. How could I have known it was blue?"

"You wore a blue dress and diamonds, and the diamonds sparkled when you turned."

Her heart began to pound. They looked at each other. Her voice was faint and filled with awe. "And there were crystal chandeliers and there was music. . . ."

"And the light was shining in your eyes when you looked up at me. We danced as though we had danced here before and would dance here again. . . ."

"I can scarcely believe this, Cody!"

He scratched his chin. "Something odd has been going on for a long time, then. Unexplainable . . ."

Ellen hurried into the ballroom, turning around and around, her arms out, losing herself in the magic of the regal space. "My gown is blue organza and silk and it's twirling, twirling under the sparkling lights! Can't you see it? Can't you see the magic?"

Cody set down the leather suitcase. "I can see it very well." And it was true. As she whirled, the dream returned, and her jeans and purple T-shirt and sneakers transformed into the filmy blue gown and silver slippers. How beautiful she was! The most beautiful woman he had ever seen. No wonder she was like a princess in his dreams.

He had known even when he was a kid that Ellen Montrose was no ordinary girl. He had known even then, without consciously knowing, that she was, in fact, a princess. A part of Ellen knew it, too. Otherwise she wouldn't be here, dancing in this elegant ballroom, in a gown that took his breath away. Remembering, he began to hear the music.

She heard it, too, so no words were needed when he approached and opened his arms. She slid into the warmth and reality of him and they fell into the rhythm of the music.

"You look beautiful in blue," he said.

"And you look magnificent in black tails."

"I know. I've always thought so."

As they twirled, she asked, "Cody, which is this? Is it a dream or is it real?"

"I don't know the difference anymore. Maybe there is no difference."

"What does that mean?"

"Maybe we live on two planes at once. We must, because we've been connecting on that other plane."

"The dream plane."

"Yeah."

"But how? Why?"

"It must have to do with love, Ellen. And destiny."

This made her shudder with fear. "Why this house? It has nothing to do with us."

"Somehow it does. Why, I don't know, but somehow it does. We can both hear the music. We both have seen the ghost. There is a reason, Ellen. It's not just coincidence. There is a reason for our dreams."

He looked down at her as they danced. She looked up to meet his eyes. Even in the dim light, they were vivid blue, like in her dreams. Like in the sunlight. *The real magic*, she thought, *is in his eyes. . . .*

"Love is the reason," Cody said. "You know that as well as I."

"I do know," her heart answered. "I do know."

His kiss was light at first, in the sparkles of the crystal chandeliers. As it deepened, she felt his heart beating against her own, and his breath finding the rhythm of her own.

Their breaths were the rhythm of the music. The spirit of the house surrounded them and wrapped them in the throbbing colors of its aura. They belonged here. The unfulfilled dreams of the house mingled with their dreams and dazzled them, dazed them, captivated them. On this summer evening the mansion was theirs.

Cody's hands combed through her hair sensually as he kissed her. Ellen tossed back her head, allowing his kisses to reach her throat. Tingles of desire shuddered through her body. Her head began to spin as it always did when Cody kissed her.

Wrapped in the magic, she thought of the dreams and how she had so desperately wanted him to stay...to touch her...to kiss her.... Now it was happening, and Cody was right; it was very hard to tell which was the dream and which was the mysterious condition called "reality."

She only knew that this time there was no danger of his disappearing. So perhaps this was the dream . . . completing itself.

"I love you, Ellen," he was whispering between soft, electric kisses. "I want you...."

Slowly they sank to the floor. The music was still there. The dance was not over; it was only beginning.

14

THE EMPTY HOUSE enfolded them, welcoming them, its haunted echoes sighing as if it had never before known lovers—as if it had been deprived of this special joy.

It was true; laughter had not dwelt here. Ellen had known it even as a child, looking at the lights come on in the few selected rooms; and she had felt sorry for the mansion then, because her heart told her that within its stately walls there was no gaiety, no joy. No love.

Love was here now, if only for a day.

With the magic surrounding them, Ellen forgot everything except the moment . . . for the moment was the touch of Cody's lips, the touch of his fingertips, the touch of his eyelashes, soft against her cheek.

Untucking his white cotton shirt from the waist of his jeans, Cody muttered, "These tuxes are damn stiff."

"Then let me help with those studs." She smiled, finding the buttons of his shirt.

Moments later her hands moved over the hard muscles of his tanned, bare chest. "How beautiful you are!" she said.

"Ah, my sweet! You are more beauty than I ever imagined." His hands slid under her T-shirt and along her bare midriff. "Beauty . . . and in that sparkling dress that matches the color of your eyes."

She looked at him. "You know my gown is blue?"

"It's as blue as the color of this room. I was there, remember? It sparkled when we were dancing, and when I felt its softness I nearly went crazy with wanting you. But I don't want to wrinkle it."

"No, we mustn't wrinkle—"

"Underneath, you are softer still." He lifted the purple T-shirt over her head. "Your softness is the miracle of you." Kissing her, he slid flat onto the floor and pulled her down to him, closer than before, closer than *ever* before. It was not that his arms held her tighter, but that his love was stronger, his need greater. And how could it not be, now that they had learned the depth of their sharing? Now that they knew this was how their ballroom dream was meant to end?

From the windows, lavender-and-silver twilight illuminated their naked bodies as shadows drifted across their borrowed world, and evening birds sang in the highest tree branches. In a blur of pleasure, Ellen accepted the sweet torment of his love—drops of fire against her skin as his lips explored, tasting the beauty, the perfume, the surging need, and the essence of her. She cried out his name, but the sound of his name came only as a whispered sigh, half plea, half wonder.

Each flame that touched her, burned words from somewhere deep inside her heart. *No other man has ever known me . . . nor ever loved me. . . . No other man ever will again . . . for there is no other.* Even in the whirlpool of passion Ellen heard the desperate cry within her— *There is no other . . . only him. . . .*

Tears of runaway emotion blurred her eyes. "Cody . . . !"

He reached up to press his hand gently, reassuringly against her breast. Her breaths became silky moans, echoing in the deep silence of the house, coming louder and faster until they erupted in a fevered shudder.

His body moved over hers like an ocean wave consuming her, drowning her, wrapping her in the celebration of itself.

The miracle of manhood...needing...possessing...giving...

Through a veil of tears, she looked up and saw, for a split second, the woman she had become as a reflection in his deep blue eyes—the woman she was this very moment, experiencing with astounding pleasure the man he was.

Quivering, breathless, drenched by the surge of his passion, Ellen accepted him as naturally and completely as she accepted the rushing and ebbing of her pulse, finding his.

His throaty moan came from behind closed eyes as his body went rigid and trembled. His hands found hers above her head and held on, as if to keep himself from falling.

In those seconds of his helplessness, Ellen felt the sensation of her love flowing into him, filling every cavern of his loneliness and every vessel of his need.

IN THE AFTERGLOW she lay in his arms, bathed in the last silver-blue of twilight chased by encroaching shadows. He wiped at a trickle of moisture on her cheek and whispered, "Why the tears? Are you sad?"

"I'm sadder and happier than I thought it possible to be."

This comment was met by a long silence, after which he said, staring at the ceiling, "So am I."

The hedging shades of night carried in with them the crisp mountain air. Cody moved closer. "Is your body really covered in powdery sparkles, or am I seeing you in angel's attire?"

She smiled. "They're sparkles of heat from your body." Her trembling had eased and now began again. "It's getting cold."

"And dark."

"Dark?" Ellen struggled up onto her elbows. "Oh, no! There's barely enough light for us to see our way out of here. How are we going to read the book and the papers?"

"We could take the suitcase with us."

"Out through the basement window? But that's like stealing. It doesn't belong to us."

"Who *does* it belong to after all these years, Ellen?"

"I— To the ghost. What if she is the spirit of the Iris Whitfield who wrote the diary? It could very well be. She must have been the one who hid the suitcase, and now she wants somebody to find it."

"The ghost definitely wanted somebody to find it," Cody said, sitting up and reaching for his clothes. "But I agree we can't just walk off with it. Tell you what—" He paused as he pulled on his jeans. "I have a flashlight in my car. I'll go down and get it while you dress."

He picked up her clothes from where they had fallen and handed them to her. "Your gown, my lady."

When he was gone, the same feeling of abandonment came over her that she had felt in the dreams. It was a ghost's house she was alone in, and there was no way of knowing when or where the specter might show herself again. Ellen hurriedly pulled on her clothes and went to the window. It was impossible to see down through the thick tree branches to the place where Cody would have parked his car.

He must have rushed all the way; before she expected him, he was standing in the ballroom holding the lighted flashlight in one hand and rubbing his shin with the other.

"I had to feel my way through the basement getting out," he said. "And ran smack into a wrought-iron chair." Quickly he moved from in front of the window. "We have to be careful to make sure nobody sees this light moving around up here."

Ellen sat down on the floor and pulled the suitcase open.

He shone the light on the contents while Ellen lifted out the box and untied the bow of blue ribbon.

Cautiously, she lifted the lid and brushed aside a layer of pale blue tissue paper. Her hand felt heavy lace. Excited, she pulled out a carefully folded white dress trimmed in pearls and lace. "It's a wedding dress!" Her fingers glided lovingly over the fabric. "It's beautiful! Do you think it belonged to her? To Iris Whitfield?"

"Likely so." Cody picked up some papers and moved them into the light beam. "This is a baptismal certificate." He read, 'Mary Helen Whitfield, born in November 1895.' Clipped to it is a hospital record of her birth."

"Obviously these people were family of the Whitfield who built the mansion. The last people who lived here weren't Whitfields. There was an old couple named Meullar." Ellen was folding the dress and replacing it gently in its box.

While she did so, Cody picked up the leather-bound notebook and flipped through to the last written page. "The final entry in the diary is April 29, 1902. That's only three months after the first entry."

Suddenly, from the white-pillared archway, the filmy presence reappeared. The ghost floated below the ceiling across the spacious room and hovered not far above them. It was almost as if she wanted to join them out of interest in what they were doing. Ellen's initial fear had evaporated with familiarity. The spirit was not hostile. In fact, this time it exuded cordiality.

"You must be Iris Whitfield," Ellen exclaimed to the floating phantom. "You led us to your diary because you wanted us to find it." The ghost was more plainly visible than ever before. Then she gradually began to fade. "We have to read the diary, Cody!"

He handed her the open notebook and focused the beam of the flashlight on the pages. Ellen tried to adjust her eyes to the delicate handwriting.

"Iris identifies herself on the first page as the second wife of Lawrence Whitfield—the man who built the mansion in

1880." She looked up. "That was the year the mine opened, so Lawrence would have been the owner of the mine."

"Second wife, you said?" Cody asked, squinting to try to see the thin scroll.

Ellen nodded, turning the page. "Oh, my." She paused. "Listen.

> "At the time of this writing my husband, Lawrence, has been dead for three long years and I know I am soon to join him in the hereafter. I shall not live to my thirtieth birthday, which is only five months away. The lung disease is fatal; I must accept that now, but I do not want to leave Mary Helen. My little daughter is not yet seven years old. She is too young to fight them for what is rightfully hers, and I am too weak. I can do little more now than write this account of the truth and hope it reaches someone who can help me before my enemies find it."

Cody frowned. "What kind of crazy drama have we stumbled onto?"

Intrigued, Ellen was already reading on.

> "My husband's first marriage ended after twenty-eight years, with his wife's death. The first Mrs. Lawrence Whitfield, before me, was named Hannah. Twelve months after Hannah's death, Lawrence and I were married at the little chapel near Rollington. He was forty-six and I was nineteen. His family did not approve of his marriage to a mine worker's daughter. He brought me to this wonderful house which I had always dreamed of from afar and never imagined I would live in. Mary Helen was born, Lawrence's only child, and we were very happy. Our daughter was only five when Law-

rence died of heart failure.

"A few months ago, I found out that Hannah's nephew from Fort Collins, who is an attorney-at-law, is planning to take the house away from me. His name is Mr. Roger Meullar and he suddenly came to my door after it became known that I am terminally ill. He asked to see my marriage license and then took it and would not return it to me. The public records burned years ago when the courthouse caught fire, and the preacher who married us has passed away. There is no way for me to prove I am legally married. Mr. Meullar has prepared a case to prove that he is legal heir to the house through his aunt Hannah. He says Lawrence never legally married me and therefore Mary Helen is not a Whitfield heir. I fear he will take the house as soon as I am gone."

Ellen looked up with horror in her eyes. "This is terrible! That poor girl!"

"And he did take the house from her, obviously," Cody said. "He was a Meullar."

Ellen remembered the old couple who lived here when she was a child. Would he have been Roger? Yes, it seemed as if that was his name. Now their granddaughter Carolyn owned the house and didn't want it. How sad . . .

She recalled the summer Carolyn Meullar came to Shadow Valley to see her grandparents and left after only a few days, telling stories around town of a ghost that haunted the mansion. To this day, it was said, Carolyn had returned only once, to collect items she wanted from the estate.

"So Carolyn encountered the ghost of the woman her grandfather took the house away from . . ." she mused.

"What?"

"Carolyn Meullar. She's the present heir and she's been trying to sell this place for more than three years. Rumors are that she's scared to death of it because of the ghost."

"A lot of people are," Cody said. "The Whitfield mansion is reputed to be not only haunted, but cursed, as well. You're the first person I've ever met who had the nerve to come in here alone."

She smiled. "Except for you."

"I've never been afraid of ghosts." He laughed.

She laughed with him. "I remember your reputation. You were never afraid of anything."

"Not stupid things like ghosts, anyhow. Ghosts are just people who are dead. There's no person I'm afraid of, dead or alive."

Ellen studied his eyes and knew that he wasn't boasting; he was merely stating the truth. The gentle side that he had always shown her was a side of Cody that few people had ever seen. He had grown up tough, with as many chips piled on his shoulder as were piled on hers, and he'd fought his way out of the stigma of a poverty-stricken childhood. Now she recognized one thing that had been plaguing her all day—Cody's reaction to the ghost. He'd shown not a trace of fear.

No wonder she felt so protected whenever he was with her. No wonder she had walked the streets of Shadow Valley and felt different, even felt people reacting in a different way. It wasn't her. It was him.

Ellen pushed the journal back into the cone of light and scanned the yellowed pages. "It gets harder and harder to read. This is a day-to-day account of injustice and Iris's desperate attempt to get someone to help her." She turned more pages. "Oh, no!"

"What is it?"

"This rotten nephew had Iris evicted! Can you imagine? A dying woman and her little girl evicted! Iris is saying that before she leaves, she is going to hide what proof she has left of her marriage inside this house. She has written a prayer on the last page that someone will find it and learn the truth. I can scarcely read the prayer, the handwriting is so weak." She turned to the last page and the end of the prayer. A cry of alarm came from her throat.

Cody moved closer—an instantaneous protective reflex—and his arm came around her shoulder. "What's wrong?"

It was a struggle to find her voice. She held out the book. "Look . . . Iris's signature on the final page. Iris Montrose Whitfield!"

"Montrose?" Cody scratched his head. *"Montrose?"*

"How can it be . . . ? Cody! My great-grandmother was named Mary Helen! Could it be that Iris—that the ghost—is the mother of that same Mary Helen?"

"If her maiden name was Montrose, yeah, it could very well be."

Ellen's mind reeled. *Could it also be that the ghost came to me in my dreams to lead me here because I am her great-great-granddaughter?* No, it was crazy! Yet her great-grandmother's name *was* Mary Helen!

Cody uncrossed his legs and rose, leaving the flashlight casting its flare like a small dagger on the dusty floor. "This could mean that Carolyn Meullar isn't the rightful heir to Whitfield mansion. You are."

"It couldn't be. . . . Things like that just don't happen. . . ." In the arrow of light, Ellen's hands trembled over the ribbon of the box that held all that was left of a young girl's dreams—a wedding dress. She imagined the day Iris Montrose wore it, with joy and hope for a sparkling future.

Ellen clutched the old diary to her chest and dissolved into tears.

She felt Cody's hand on her shoulder. "Honey, let's go. We're going to take the case with us. Everything else in the house might legally belong to Carolyn Meullar, but this sure as hell doesn't. These documents need to be looked at more closely."

Night had closed in; darkness sat thick and heavy in the mansion. Careful that the flashlight beam not show in any of the windows, Cody led her down the flights of stairs, holding her arm and carrying the leather suitcase. The basement was as black as a cave. He helped her climb outside, handed up the case, and followed, closing the window.

Buster materialized out of a clump of weeds. He had been amusing himself chasing field mice while he waited for Cody. Ellen was glad for this friendly reminder of what life had been before she entered the mansion tonight. She was grateful Cody had driven his car, because most of the strength had drained out of her body. Her legs had gone numb from the shock, and the last thing she wanted to do was pick her way home through the dark of a moonless night, even with Buster as a scout.

"I don't want to go home," she said. "I can't bear the dreariness of Pebble Street tonight, thinking about the generations of my family—all the women of my family—who lived there and never got away, even when they tried."

Cody nodded in understanding and headed toward the radio station. "I have a show to do in an hour. We'll find something to drink and a snack, and you can make yourself comfortable in my luxury digs while I entertain the thriving metropolis of Shadow Valley."

Ellen thought of his sexy deep voice coming over the airwaves and experienced a surge of pride. "Everyone does listen to you," she said. "They talk about the program changes."

"I wonder how many have noticed my continuing semisubtle endeavor to change their musical tastes."

She laughed. "You're bringing class to this old mountain town."

"Damn right." He grinned. "Just like you do. Two pebbles polished into gemstones." As they turned onto the main thoroughfare and drove under the streetlights, he turned to her. "We're going to investigate this thing."

His words caused a rumble more of fear than excitement; she wasn't sure why. Fear of hoping? Fear of it being true? "Oh, but Cody, this happened nearly a century ago. All these people are long dead."

"Iris Montrose is still living in the mansion. Still hoping to find vindication."

Maybe this, too, is a dream, she thought, reaching over to touch his arm. "Promise me secrecy. Any inquiries we make must be done carefully. It wouldn't do for people all over town to start saying I'm trying to claim I'm an heir to the mansion. The story is just too far-fetched. And if Iris couldn't get help then, when she actually was Lawrence Whitfield's living wife, what chance would there be for a distant heir? If I even *am* her heir?"

He shrugged. "I dunno. For one thing, scheming Roger is long dead."

Later, while she sat on Cody's bed with Buster, listening to his live broadcast from the studio down the hall, Ellen remembered her grandfather's family Bible. Dog-eared and limp, it had been passed down for generations. Family births and deaths had been recorded in that Bible, possibly as far back as her grandfather's grandmother. In fact, she realized, this was where she had heard of Mary Helen Montrose. Her name was in the family Bible.

They got out the Bible when he took her home after the broadcast. Ellen would not stay the night at his station apartment; people would notice and the town would talk. Even if she would soon be away from here forever, she refused to give them anything to gossip about. And it wouldn't be so good for Cody, either, even though he didn't seem to care.

Anyway, she had to get up early and work on the dresses. It felt wonderful to be away from the truck stop, putting her own talents to use. Her cherished career had actually begun to take shape.

It was a night of little sleep. She hadn't wanted to let on to Cody how truly rattled she was about this strange turn of events. Mary Helen had apparently not even been allowed to retain the Whitfield name, but in the Bible someone had marked a *W.* after the entry of her name.

BY THE END OF THE WEEK, all the evidence was in the hands of an attorney. A search for public records had turned up nothing. They had only the accusation of an ill and bitter woman that could never be verified. Iris's journal might be true, the attorney said, but there was no way of proving it after so many years. He assured them that no case could be opened. The matter could get no further.

Ellen hid her disappointment the way she had learned to hide so many of her feelings. She hadn't dared hope, anyway. After all, her dreams had been of a magnificent house; this one was run-down. Her destination couldn't ever have been a haunted, neglected place; her destination was a career of dazzling success.

"You never really believed it could be, did you?" Cody asked, as they sat at lunch in the Silver Nugget.

She shook her head and smiled. "Me own a mansion? Well, if I ever do, it won't be a dusty, weed-grown one." As she said it, something tugged at her heart. The house, like Iris Whitfield, deserved a better fate. It was like a living thing to her and, yes, she would have given anything if it had been hers, whether she ever admitted it or not.

A chain of events that happened during the following week jolted Ellen, and reminded her of her private determination to escape Shadow Valley. On Tuesday, Cody learned from one of the town council members that an offer had been accepted on the mansion from a buyer in Denver who planned to convert it to a hotel. The news hit Ellen hard—that this should be the final chapter in the struggle of Iris Montrose Whitfield to claim her rightful home. The mansion seemed doomed never to be a home to anyone again.

This news was bad enough. Even worse was what happened on Wednesday night.

Cody had stayed late at her house on Tuesday, languishing in bed drinking Burgundy wine, and when they had made love, Ellen's heart kept crying that she could never leave him; she loved him too much. For days she had known that she was lingering because Cody was here. Her confused heart didn't know how to explain it to her equally confused head.

At her insistence, he had not slept over, but left her to the reality of the silent empty house on Pebble Street and her plans to rise very early to finish Doreen Engleson's dress.

Around nine the next morning, she was carefully ironing the last seams when Jed Mortimer phoned from the truck-stop café.

"Can you do me a big favor, Ellen? Can you come in to work? I'm short of help the next two nights because Millie is off to a cousin's wedding in Estes. I haven't found a replacement for you yet. It's not gonna be easy."

It would be hard to say no after all the favors Jed had done for her over the years, even though Ellen had made all the emotional disconnections from her identity as a waitress at a truck stop. It would cut into her deadline for completing the two other dresses. It would also be an excuse to prolong making her plans for leaving, at least for a couple more days.

"Okay," she heard herself say. "The usual shift?"

"Yeah. I appreciate this."

"No problem. I'll see you tonight."

Ellen looked over the gown; it was as superb as she'd envisioned. Doreen Engleson would be very pleased.

DOREEN WAS PLEASED to the point of raving. Cody had volunteered to take Ellen in his car to deliver the gown so she wouldn't have to carry it. He sat outside and waited until Ellen bounced out with a check in her hands.

"The honorable mayor's wife is ecstatic," Ellen said, getting into his car.

"You knew she'd be happy. You have an amazing talent."

"I know. I really do know. The other dresses I'm commissioned for will be stunning, too."

Cody looked at his watch as he drove toward the town's business district. It was nearly one-thirty. "Do you want me to drop you at the café?"

"No, I want to deposit this check, and I know you need to get to work yourself. I'll stop at the bank and walk from there."

He pulled up in front of the bank building. "I'll meet you when you get off, then. Around eleven?"

"Thanks." Ellen smiled and squeezed his hand. "See you then."

IT STARTED OUT AS AN ordinary evening at the Blue Spruce. Customers were talking about the unusually warm weather. The atmosphere began to change when Harvey Altman walked in.

When he saw Ellen, the heavily built local trucker adjusted his brimmed cap and grinned. "Well, look who's back. Hail the princess."

If Millie had been here, Ellen could have refused to wait on Harvey, but tonight there was no choice. The best she could do as a way of protest was to keep him waiting. When she did walk to his table, she handed him the menu, avoiding his gaze.

"They said you quit."

"Why would you care, one way or the other?"

"Hey! For the last seven years you've been the prettiest part of this place—a fixture, like. Then all of a—"

Not wanting to hear what else the man had to say, Ellen interrupted, "I'll be back to take your order," and turned on her heel. Her reactions to Harvey Altman were familiar; he had been giving her a hard time since they were kids at school. Millie insisted Altman acted that way because he'd had a crush on Ellen for years and she wouldn't give him so much as a smile.

Taking an order while deflecting snide or suggestive comments was a skill Ellen had perfected long ago. Altman had something on his mind, but he wasn't about to get a chance to say it. Not a man to allow a woman to get the better of him, Altman sat sulking in the booth for more than an hour while Cody's voice and Cody's music filled the room. Twice, Ellen turned up the radio.

As the hour grew later, the customers thinned out. Altman waved for more coffee—his sixth refill. When she took too long to bring it, he yelled across the room, "Hey, Pebble Princess! You gonna bring my coffee or not?"

The other customers turned to look. Fuming, Ellen lifted the coffeepot from the burner, wishing she could pour it over Altman's greasy head. While she filled his mug he grinned. "Jed said you quit. What happened? Did your good-lookin' meal ticket dump you for a society gal and send you packin'? Found out what side of the tracks is what in this town, did he? *After* he had his bit of fun, though—according to what people are sayin'."

Ellen continued to ignore him until she saw that Harvey's eyes had fixed themselves on something behind her, and the eyes were staring, dumbfounded.

She whirled around. Cody!

15

ELLEN STEPPED BACK in fright. Cody's face, contorted with rage, explicitly answered her urgent question—and Harvey Altman's. He had heard everything the trucker had said.

So deep was her fear of Cody's wrath, no sound came from her lips when she tried to say his name. Dread mixed with ineffable emotions of another kind, too—the savory anticipation of revenge.

The silence was terrible and seemed to last forever, but in actuality it was only seconds before Cody reached the table. Every head in the place was turned toward him. "Do you want to repeat what you just said or is it only ladies you insult to their faces?"

The barely controlled fury in Cody's voice seemed to have a paralyzing effect on Harvey Altman. Gripping his coffee mug, he opened his mouth and squawked, "I ain't said nothin' insulting about you—I was talking about her.... Hell, everybody knows—"

A strangling sound emitted from his throat as Cody grabbed him by the shirt collar. "Everybody knows *what?*"

"Who...who...ach..." Altman's eyes went wild as he felt himself being lifted from the chair.

Jed Mortimer came bolting from the kitchen in a panic, yelling, "Hey! Hey! Take it easy!"

Altman's words bounced off Cody's rage like rain off a hot tin roof. The trucker had managed to make him even more furious, if that was possible. Jaw clenched, Cody yanked the other man out of the booth.

The first blow to Harvey's jaw sent him reeling backward, crashing into one of the tables. Jed yelled for someone to call the police. Ellen cried out Cody's name, knowing nothing she said—nothing anyone said—was going to penetrate.

Harvey sputtered through a mouth full of blood and sprang into self-defense. The large man—taller and broader than Cody—regained his balance and started forward, tossing obscenities, but no one could miss the spark of pure fear in his eyes. Cody's intense stare was enough to send terror through the veins of everyone who witnessed it. Even Jed drew back in fright.

Before Harvey could make a decision whether to run or try to defend himself, he was hit with a second blow, and then a third. All the customers were on their feet, moving away from the crashing tables as the big trucker fell backward, scattering chairs. Both hands went up in front of him—a signal for his assailant to stop.

Instead, Cody moved in closer, grabbed him once again by the jacket collar, and dragged him toward the door. Jed, perspiring, leapt forward to open it. Harvey, like a captured animal, began loudly protesting.

Outside, under the blinking red neon sign and the post lights of the parking lot, Cody forced the other man against the side of a truck. "You've needed to have your mouth shut for you for a long time!" he growled through clenched teeth.

Altman, having had time to gain his second wind, suddenly pulled free and sent a blow to the side of Cody's face—a mistake he should not have made.

By the time the police arrived three minutes later, Cody was standing over a crumpled form on the pavement.

Joe Garry was first on the scene. "What's going on?"

Jed ran toward him, hoping to avoid anything else that would set off Cody's anger. "It's just a misunderstanding!"

Cody wiped his hand across his mouth, stepped over Harvey Altman and said calmly, "Misunderstanding, hell. Harvey was long overdue for a lesson in respect."

The other officer, Mark Dickens, who had known Altman for years, helped the groaning man to his feet. Bleeding and bent over in pain, he would not look at Cody.

"What started it?" Mark asked.

Cody met the officer's eyes. "He shot off his mouth."

Joe Garry made a survey of the faces in the small crowd. He asked the café owner, "Jed, what about damage to your place? Are you going to press charges?"

Jed glanced at Ellen, then at Cody—fearfully. "No. No need. It's minimal damage."

This was a relief, but not a surprise to Ellen. It was possible Jed knew more than she thought about what she put up with from the likes of Harvey Altman. She stood back in the shadows, smothered in humiliation, not wanting to call attention to herself and not knowing what to say to Cody. The memory flashed of another time this had happened—years ago when she was eight and he was twelve. It was the same thing then as now—his anger triggered for the same reason. The difference was, he barely knew her then. This time, it was very personal for him.

Harvey was helped to the police car to be driven to the first-aid station at the hospital. He would know as well as everybody else that word of this fight would be spread all over town by tomorrow. And the reason for it, too.

The reason for it. The indignity and shame. Ellen fought back the tears that stung behind her eyes. Years of humiliation had come to a head, and in such a horrid way—Cody fighting her battle for her because it had turned out to be his battle, as well. Because of his close association with her. It didn't matter that he was originally a child of Pebble Street. He wasn't from Pebble Street now, as far as this damned town was concerned. But she was. She always would be. Even Meredith couldn't change that.

The crowd quickly dispersed, at Jed Mortimer's prompting, many of them returning inside to finish their meals. Soon Ellen was standing alone under the flickering light, watching Cody cross the parking lot toward her. His walk was unhurried. When he stood in front of her, he said nothing, merely held out his hand, and she reached back for his. They walked hand in hand down the hill, away from the Blue Spruce Truck Stop toward the sprinkle of lights of the town, and Ellen knew it was the last time. She would never go back to that place again.

He was uncharacteristically quiet as they walked the familiar, tree-lined sidewalk.

Ellen said, "I'm sorry, Cody."

He turned. "Sorry for what?"

"Sorry that you got into that violent fight because of me."

"It wasn't a fight. Harvey got in one mediocre lick when I stopped paying attention for a minute. One smack doesn't constitute a fight."

"But it was because of me."

She couldn't see his face in the darkness, but she could hear amusement in his voice. "Who else would it be because of?"

"Oh, Cody . . ."

He squeezed her hand tighter. "I'm glad I got there when I did. Ellen, has this bastard talked to you like that before?"

"He's always been a jerk with a smart mouth, but tonight was the worst. I know why, though. I never went out, never dated. Now that everybody knows you and I are close, he thought it gave him the right to razz me about . . . it."

"Gave him the right? The fool wants you for himself—anybody could see it."

"I know," she said. "Which is why he always gave me such a hard time."

Cody sighed, still forcing back rage. "I guarantee it won't ever happen again. Not Harvey nor anybody will want to take me on again. Nobody will talk to my lady with anything but respect. Ever."

Ellen walked at his side in wounded silence.

They reached the deserted town center. By the light of a streetlamp Cody saw the shine of tears on her cheeks. He stopped. "I'm sorry. I know I behaved like a savage tonight, but there are some things that can't be dealt with any other way. I couldn't blame you for being ashamed of me."

"How could I ever be ashamed of you?" she asked. "You are everything a woman ever dreams of. I will never in my lifetime meet anyone else like you—a man who would protect me with his life. A man who has even shared dreams with me."

"A man who loves you," he added. "Like I told you once before, finding you was like finding a lost part of myself."

"Oh, please don't say that! Don't!"

His arm came around her shoulder. "Ellen, what's the matter?"

She began to sob. "Don't you see? Tonight reminded me of a thousand other times . . . a thousand other jabs and remarks . . . a thousand stares and whispers behind my back. The only difference was that tonight you were there."

His voice was caring. "I'll *always* be there."

"But that's just the point. You can't be. You can't be behind my back every minute, listening to the sneers and whispers. And why should you have to be, anyhow? You have a life to build here. And you can because they don't know who you are—and even if they did, they're afraid of you now. And they respect you." She wiped tears from her cheeks with the back of her hand. "I'm going to find respect, too, because I must. I have to. But I can't do it here, and you know it. Tonight should prove it."

"It was just one guy," he argued weakly.

"It's a whole town, you know that. To them I'm white trash. Harvey Altman just has a louder voice than the others."

He didn't like the way she was talking. Obviously the Tarot cards hadn't been enough to sway her. Meredith had phoned him in a panic soon after the reading, worried about the cards Ellen had drawn, mentioning the burning Tower and saying he had to stop her plans.

Stop Ellen? Hell, he was trying, but how could he undo in a few weeks what Shadow Valley had done over years?

They walked in silence until they reached Pebble Street with its gnarled darkness and its sediment of gloom. He knew Ellen felt the gloom as much as he did.

Her porch light was the only one on. They walked into its dull yellow glow and up the paint-chipped steps. "I need a drink," he said.

"I thought you might."

A few minutes later when they were sitting at her kitchen table with glasses of gin and tonic, Ellen looked across at Cody's eyes. They were gray tonight; the blue was gone. She took a long swallow of the drink, choking it down, as if that would make it any easier to hold back the pain.

She began hesitantly, "Cody, I've told you how it's been with me. Every day, every minute of my life since I can remember, my whole focus has been my plan to get out of here. I had to stay because of my grandfather, but in my mind and my heart, every daydream was the same. The thought of leaving you tears me apart, but my staying would eventually tear both of us apart because I will never accept being called white trash."

Sitting back in the old captain's chair, he gazed at her and said nothing, only picked up his glass and took a long, slow drink.

Her eyes brimmed with tears. "Please tell me you understand."

Damn! he thought. More drastic measures were called for.
He'd have to resort to plan B: accepting an invitation from
the mayor's daughter, who had been after him since he first
hit town. Maybe seeing him with another woman would jolt
Ellen into realizing she didn't want to lose him. What did he
have to lose by trying?

Ellen was bothered by the look in his eyes. "Cody?"

"What I *don't* understand," he said finally, "is how you can
leave *me*." He scowled. "Which is the disguise, Ellen? The
woman ruled by hate for the town, or the woman ruled by
love for me?"

His anger hurt. Ellen gazed at the faded blue-and-yellow
wallpaper of the kitchen where she had spent so many hours
of her life and remembered her grandmother here at this very
table, smiling as she brought out a box of buttons and thread
and colored ric-rac and a fifteen-cent blouse from a Goodwill store. *We'll disguise it—no one will know where it came
from.... A spasm of fear hit hard. She remembered the Fool.
And the nine of Swords. Will I be in disguise for the rest of
my life?*

No! her wiser self protested. *It is here I'm in disguise! I am
not white trash!*

Cody was drinking steadily on a long day of work and an
empty stomach. He had intended to eat after he picked up
Ellen, before the damn fight ruined the evening. The liquor
had gone straight to his brain, along with his anger, and had
overpowered his built-in censors. He began to dwell on the
gypsy's prediction that Ellen would, indeed, leave him.
Pouring himself another gin and tonic, he said recklessly,
"Not many women could wave off the fact that we danced
together in our dreams because a spirit was beckoning us
both. How much proof do you need that you belong with me?

The burning Tower is a message of disaster if you go. It can even indicate career failure. I looked it up."

Ellen stared at him. "The burning Tower?"

The realization of what he'd said, stung like a swarm of wasps. "I'm speaking symbolically," he offered weakly.

Her stare penetrated. "You've talked to Meredith?"

"About what?"

"Meredith told you about the cards? Behind my back? I didn't know you two had a confidential relationship. What the devil is going on?"

"It was just a chance meeting at Mrs. Volken's." Cody wished he could think more clearly. He felt he was saying the wrong things.

"You were at the gypsy's? To have your fortune read?"

"Yeah. And to ask about the ghost in my dreams. She even pulled up the name Iris, now that I recall, but Iris wouldn't cooperate with her to give any more information. Mrs. Volken had a strong sense you shouldn't be at the Whitfield mansion, though."

Ellen's unease grew stronger by the second. "What else did she say about me?"

"That you would leave me."

"Not what you wanted to hear."

"Hell, no." Cody poured another drink.

"But the Tarot reading. That must have pleased you."

"It did."

"You knew ahead of time Meredith was going to read the cards, didn't you? I'll bet it was your idea."

"It was a good idea." He knocked back half the glass. "Now you know what to expect."

Trembling, Ellen studied him. Cody's eyes had gone very dark, which meant his thoughts were dark. Too dark. Her voice shook. "You'd do anything to stop me, wouldn't you? Would you even seduce my best friend into betraying me?"

"For your information, my sweet, Meredith wants you to stay as much as I do. If you weren't so caught up in your own feelings, you'd have more appreciation for those who care for you."

"So it was a conspiracy—that Tarot reading. Meredith fell under your spell just like I did and let you talk her into...into making up those awful predictions." Tears formed in Ellen's eyes. Her heart felt as if it were tearing apart. "How could she do that to me? How could you both?"

He glanced away to hide the fear that was building in his gut. Something in the cards had horrified Meredith. Maybe she hadn't faked all of the warning. The scheme had backfired and he'd cost Meredith her cherished friendship. He had cost himself even more. Damn it. Why didn't Ellen stop looking at him that way?

"And the leak about my making Doreen's gown? You were the only one who knew, the only one who could have told. Did you figure I might stay if I had a chance to make dresses for the local snobs?"

"There's no point in my denying it, I guess. What's one more nail in my coffin?"

Her tears were flowing freely now. The death of trust was agonizing. "I had no idea you were so underhanded."

"I said I'd do anything to keep you. Some women would be flattered." He knew he was still doing it—saying the wrong thing because there wasn't any right thing to say.

"Flattered at being tricked and lied to?"

"You might give me a chance to explain."

"Is there anything to explain that I don't already know?"

He thought about it, his head whirling, hating the pain of her tears. "I can't think of anything," he replied miserably.

"Then there is nothing more to say, is there?"

"Nothing I haven't already said." He rose, none too steadily. "I can understand why you're overcome with hurt right now. But I'm not sorry we tried to stop you. Someday you'll look back and realize how wrong you were to give me up. You'll never find what I could have given you."

Trust would have been nice, Ellen wanted to shout, but the words would have come out as sobs. Her dreams—her precious dreams—she had to hang on to them...didn't she? Who could she really trust except herself?

Cody slammed the door behind him. Numb with pain, Ellen ran upstairs and took solace, as she had always done, in her work. The last two gowns were nearly completed. She couldn't even confront Meredith because the Calhouns were at the Seattle conference. Maybe it was just as well that they wouldn't have another scene of tears to remember.

AS THE BUS PULLED OUT of Shadow Valley, Ellen sat numbly, gazing at the familiar streets, surprised at how hard it had been to walk out of the house for the last time and just close the door. Some of the furniture had sold, the rest she left, as others had left behind part of their lives on Pebble Street. In a matter of hours she would be on the plane from Denver to New York. The thrill of a lifetime. It was supposed to feel better than this.

Cody didn't know she was leaving this soon. He would have wanted to say goodbye, but she couldn't. She didn't know how.

The bus passed the Whitfield mansion, silent and despondent in the summer sun.

16

THE IMPORT APPAREL warehouse was noisy and congested. Ellen worked with three other young women on the ground floor where crates, trucked in daily from the docks, were unloaded. Her job was unpacking boxes and hanging the garments on conveyers that took them to sorters on the upper floor. The clothes were made on assembly lines in countries far away. On the job, she wore jeans and a tank top because the warehouse was hot.

Ellen's beautiful wardrobe hung in her half of a narrow closet of a walk-up flat in Hell's Kitchen, shared with one of her fellow workers. The chic suits, worn for interviews when she first came, were in their plastic garment bags.

New York was nothing like she'd imagined, but surely things would get better when she got a foothold. It had taken four weeks to find a job. After applying at fashion houses and retail stores where the wages weren't enough to live on, she had grabbed the import-house offer in desperation. Rents were so high she was afraid of exhausting her savings. Luckily a co-worker, Jennifer, was looking for someone to share her small apartment—a forty-minute subway ride from work. It was cramped and the walls were full of cracks, but the beds were comfortable.

Sometimes she went with Jennifer to a bar full of young people, but felt so out of her element it was impossible to relax and act like everybody else. This wasn't what she'd so carefully groomed herself for.

The two young women lounged in their living room one Saturday morning, drinking coffee, while Ellen looked through the Help Wanted ads in the paper—still hopeful.

"What are you looking for?" Jennifer asked. "You won't likely find anything that pays better than what we've got—with no impressive experience under your belt."

"I was naive enough to believe I could be hired on to work as an assistant designer."

Jennifer dipped her finger into her thick, milky coffee, stirred, and licked the finger thoughtfully. "Why not try out for the Broadway stage? You got just about the same chance. I wonder how many thousands of girls like you come to the city with big dreams about the fashion world."

Ellen closed the want-ad section. "I admit I'm green. But I'll learn my way around. I'm not the kind to give up."

On the floor with her back propped against a worn couch, Jennifer helped herself to the last sweet roll in the bakery sack. She was a pretty, dark-eyed woman, just twenty-one, who wore her dark hair in a long braid. Chewing, she said, "Waffle, my first roommate, gave up her actress dreams after six months. She went back to the little town in West Virginia where she came from and married her high-school sweetheart who worked in his father's appliance store."

"With a name like Waffle, what could she expect?"

"She had a big wedding in the church where she was baptized and says she wants three kids." Jennifer wiped sticky hands on her jeans. "It's not a bad thing, you know,"

"What isn't?"

"Marriage and kids. As opposed to the frustrating search for Mr. Right. Did you have a guy back in Colorado?"

Ellen's heart tugged. "Yes. But I wouldn't do a Waffle and go crawling back. I've severed all ties."

"Me, too, but I'm not so far from home—Atlantic Beach. You know, Long Island. I didn't get along with my mom and stepdad, so I moved out." She spread out her arms and tossed back her head. "So here we are! Living the good life!"

Marriage and kids, Ellen thought. Would Cody be a father someday? Of course, he would. He wanted the best life had to offer. And she . . . ? Marriage had never been in the dream. *But Cody would be a father someday.*

Jennifer straightened. "Hey! Are you crying? You *are!* You're homesick!"

"I could never be homesick."

"Don't tell me. I know all the symptoms. Come on, admit it. Just now, you were thinking about your house—"

"My house isn't there anymore," Ellen said defensively. Jennifer was working up to a "diversion." It was Saturday and she wanted to go to a singles club to meet men. "Better than sitting here homesick," Jennifer was about to argue.

"What do you mean, your house isn't there anymore? Did somebody buy it?"

"Yes. But not to live in. To convert to a hotel."

"Whoa! It must be a helluva big house!"

Ellen nodded. "Sometimes I wish I hadn't lost it."

Her roommate was on her feet by now. "I know just the remedy for homesick blues. How about coming with me to Errol's Dock? It's a good crowd over there on Saturday."

Ellen threw aside the paper, calling up her reserve of optimism. "Okay, sure." This was New York, after all. And she had a few friends and a place to live and a job. It was just a matter of time before the magic started happening. . . .

ELLEN HAD BELIEVED the dreams had stopped, but that night Ellen dreamed about the mansion and Cody.

The house was no longer splendid; it was dark and full of cobwebs. Cody sat in the dining room. She could see him through the French doors and he looked beautiful. She wanted in, but the doors were latched. At the sound of her knocking on the glass, he turned and looked at her with strange eyes and he would not get up to open the doors.

The crystal chandeliers rattled. Ellen looked up. The crystals were made of cobwebs. The house was no longer welcoming. A moment later Cody was gone and the ghost, no longer friendly, hovered near the ceiling.

Perspiration drenched Ellen when she awoke. The flat was stuffy and hot, but it was the dream that caused her discomfort. She and Cody shared that dream, she was certain, as they had shared the others—but this time, in the gloom and dust of discarded hopes. Had he wakened at the same instant? Was he lying in his room this very moment, thinking of that awful dream and of her?

She sat up, brushing her hair from her eyes. Noise came from the living room—the music and voices of partying. No one had been here when she went to bed. Jen had stayed on at the club after Ellen left; friends must have come home with her.

Sitting in the darkened room, Ellen cursed the ghost. "Leave me alone, Iris," she whispered. "There is nothing I can do and there never was. So please just leave me alone."

But memories of Cody wouldn't leave. He had written a letter after she'd sent her address to Jed Mortimer for her tax return, apologizing for trying to trick her. Meredith had written, too, devastated, saying there had been a terrible misunderstanding. Ellen had answered both letters impersonally and politely, not letting on that New York was a disappointment.

She pulled on jeans and a shirt, washed her face and went to join Jennifer's late-night party in the living room. She was greeted enthusiastically by the four young people, two of whom she had met before. The air smelled of popcorn and cigarettes and Jennifer's stale air-freshener.

"So . . . she emerges!"

Ellen helped herself to a handful of popcorn from a bowl on the table. "I needed a nap."

Her roommate made introductions. A man named Dave asked what she wanted to drink, as if she were a guest and he the host, and proceeded to the kitchen to tap into the wine supply. In moments he was back, handing her a glass.

"Thank you," she said, and sat down on the floor.

Dave sat beside her. "I saw you at the club with Jen. You left early. Don't you like Errol's Dock?"

"I like Errol's fine," she replied. "It's just so different from anything I'm used to. I'm nursing a minor case of culture shock."

"Jen says you're from Colorado. Denver?" She shook her head. "No. A little town in the heart of the Rockies. And you? New York?"

"Vermont. But I've lived here six years. I work for an advertising agency." He took a drink from his mug of beer. "I hope you won't hold it against me, but I queried Jen about you when I found out you were her new roommate."

Ellen gave him a sideways glance. "Oh? And what did she tell you?"

"That you two work together at the warehouse but you're looking to get into fashion design. That you don't talk about yourself much. She thinks you ran away from home."

She laughed. "Ran away? At age twenty-four?"

Dave, a well-built young man in his early thirties, wore expensive slacks and a silk shirt and smelled of success. "Well, you know Jennifer. She thinks you came to New York to escape an arranged marriage."

"Where on earth would she get that idea?"

He shrugged and waited for her to volunteer the truth, but instead, Ellen withdrew into silence, listening to the music. "You're a woman of mystery," Dave teased.

She shook her head and smiled, offering him a dish of peanuts from the cluttered coffee table. "You're just trying to keep from talking about yourself."

"Not a bit. Start me talking about myself and I don't turn off." He grabbed a handful of the peanuts. "Jennifer might be off the mark, but not too far, I don't think. Why does a girl who obviously comes from wealth appear in New York City with only the clothes she can carry—clothes, incidentally, that Jen says cause her eyes to bulge?"

Ellen stared at him, stunned.

The man shifted his position and leaned closer so as not to be heard by the others, who were talking noisily all around them. "Uh-oh. I can see I'm getting too personal. Damn me. When I'm as curious about a woman as I am about you— Let me rephrase that. When I want to get to know someone as much as I would like to know you . . . I tend to jump in like a miser after leprechaun gold. I'm observant. I'm trained to be. You might not wear any jewelry, Miss Montrose, but one can't hide breeding under jeans and a baggy shirt. I know an aristocrat when I meet one."

A feeling of peace came over Ellen, like none she had felt in her life. She reveled in the reverberation of those words— *I know an aristocrat when I see one.* "So do I—know an aristocrat when I see one."

This brought a grin. "All right. We've established we have something in common. My folks even talked about an arranged marriage once with the daughter of some business tycoon in England. So in my own fashion, I ran away, too, after college, to do my own thing. I won't quiz you anymore. Not right now, anyhow. Maybe someday." He looked up suddenly as if he had just thought of something. "It wasn't an escape from a mean husband, was it?"

"Certainly not." She sipped the wine, feeling giddy. A major victory had been won! She had tried so hard to shed the stigma of "low birth" that she had pulled it off even better than she could have imagined was possible. And done it here in the city without even trying. *Can one wear a disguise all one's life?* she remembered asking herself. *Could she?*

It didn't matter right now. An aristocrat believed she was one of his own, and that was the realization of a dream.

Curling her legs under her, Ellen said, "The past is over. Let's not talk about the past."

THIS TUXEDO WAS NOT imaginary. It was purchased from a firm in Denver. The ballroom wasn't in a lonely, dusky mansion; it was on the top floor of the Shadow Valley Hotel. Cody could feel eyes turn his way as he entered. He could even hear a few gasps that confirmed what his mirror had told him—he looked damned fine in the first tux he'd ever owned. There were whispers, too, and he knew why. The town's most eligible bachelor had arrived at the lavish autumn ball without a lady on his arm.

The truth was, he hadn't wanted to come, but in his capacity as the newly appointed city manager, it was an unspoken requirement. Anyone who *was* anyone in the whole of the county made certain not to miss Shadow Valley's social event of the year. Besides, he had some important contacting to do, business to discuss. Many major deals had often been made with the clink of champagne glasses.

He recognized Ellen's three gowns at once. Even if he hadn't known who had purchased them, he could have picked out those that eclipsed every other dress at the huge gathering. Ellen would swell with pride if she were here....

Women were trying to catch his eye, and being quite obvious about it. Because this was such a formal affair, they would be less inclined to take the initiative of asking him to dance, which was good. Ever since Ellen left he had been pursued by a dozen women, not all of whom were young or single. He wasn't interested. It was too soon after Ellen. Maybe it would always be too soon after Ellen.

He made his way to the bar and ordered a drink just as he was approached by the honorable mayor and his wife. "Glad you could make the party," Ben Engleson said, gripping Cody's shoulder as a father would his son's.

Cody greeted them both. Doreen stepped forward in Ellen's magnificent lavender gown. "Congratulations, Cody! My word, after only three weeks with you as city manager, this whole town is changing. I can't tell you how excited I am about your Pebble Street project! Absolutely brilliant—turning what has been Shadow Valley's disgrace into what will be one of its greatest assets. Whatever gave you the idea?"

"I took a good look at the place," Cody replied, accepting his drink from the bartender. "And saw its potential. The original brick street, the enormous trees, the quaintness of the miners' houses—what's left of them."

The woman's eyes shone. "It had never occurred to any of us that people might *want* to live in the restored—"

"I know the people to attract," he interrupted.

The mayor grinned proudly. "Which is the amazing thing, Doreen. Cody knows where to find them."

Doreen cooed, "Artists. Writers. Retired people who want the atmosphere. Your campaign has been brilliant."

People talked of little else these days. Cody had managed to rally the entire town in his determination to restore Pebble Street with the quaint mining-village ambience it once had. Donations and city funding had already been put to use in cleaning up the area, tearing down what buildings couldn't be saved, clearing out weeds, landscaping. Brick planters filled with fall flowers had been placed along the center of the street, which was closed to traffic. Three houses had already been purchased by outsiders and were being rebuilt according to new city requirements for authenticity.

"Who knows?" Ben Engleson said. "We might even go so far as to get a few local citizens to move down there."

"Locals? I doubt it," his wife blurted out.

Cody smiled. "I've decided to move there myself and work on a house restoration. I'm negotiating a deal before the properties get too expensive. I was interested in the Montrose house, but it was the first home to sell."

Two or three other people standing nearby were openly eavesdropping on the conversation. He had been the one to mention the name Montrose. "Where *is* Ellen?" Doreen asked.

"New York. Didn't she tell you?"

"She mentioned it once. But such a sudden decision. Do you hear from her?"

"She's been hired by a fashion firm. With her talent and her credentials, she had her choice of positions."

"I can imagine!" Doreen glanced down at the gown she was wearing, smoothing the skirt with arrogance. It prompted him to invite her to dance.

This was a mistake, because once he had shown his willingness to get out on the dance floor, the jostling for his attention began, starting with Doreen's daughter, Joanna, who had arrived just in time to see her mother dancing with the handsome man of the hour.

After a few obligatory dances, he made his way across the crowded room, and caught the sound of Ellen's name at the same moment he was waylaid by Jeff Calhoun.

Jeff thrust out his hand and began a conversation, but Cody was only half listening. His ears were tuned to voices behind him discussing Ellen. "That girl wouldn't have left *him*," a woman was saying. "He got in over his head before he realized she was Pebble Street. What'd he expect, picking up a waitress at a truck stop?"

Cody felt hot under the collar in the stiff tux, as anger began to rise.

"New in town . . ." another woman said. "Lucky for him he didn't get stuck . . . reputation . . . Pebble Street . . ."

The words became muffled and hard to hear, but he had heard enough. This was the source of Ellen's anguish over a town that meant to keep her under their boot soles. Even now, when she was gone, they kept it up. It was time to set the record straight.

He winked at Jeff, the only person in Shadow Valley who knew the truth of Cody's origins, and turned around to the small cluster of women—the "in" group of socialites, the ones who had been competing with each other in clothes and trips and husbands' incomes since high school.

"Did I hear somebody mention Ellen's name?" he asked. The animosity did not show in his voice; he sounded as engagingly pleasant as ever.

The faces turned crimson in unison. No one spoke.

He persisted. "I heard somebody call her a Pebble Street kid. Exactly what does that mean?"

"Just that . . . she came from that part of town."

"Is that significant?"

Another woman spoke up, encouraged by the fact that he seemed genuinely interested. "People actually live in those shabby houses—" She was interrupted by a nudge from a companion, meant to remind her of his "affair" with Ellen Montrose. She flushed, then recovered, determined to make the proper impression on the new city official.

Before Cody could respond, he felt pressure on his arm from Jeff Calhoun. "His Honor the Mayor asked you to make a little speech, right, Cody?"

He turned around to meet his friend's amused gaze, and nodded. The timing couldn't be better.

Jeff grinned. "They're gathering at the platform to do the usual rituals of patting themselves on the back."

Cody tugged at his uncomfortable, sweat-soaked collar, adjusted his bow tie, and made his way through the crowd to the platform where city officials were standing like penguins at feeding time. Although he hadn't been through one of these ceremonies, it didn't take much imagination to anticipate the procedure.

"Where's Meredith?" he asked. "I wouldn't want her to miss my performance."

"She's here somewhere. I'll find her."

Cody took his place beside the other officials and stood listening to their praises of the town and each other until he was called on. When his name with his new title was announced, the applause was overwhelming and lasted until he raised an arm to stop it.

"I thank you," he said. "And I appreciate your support. Shadow Valley is on the way to fulfilling its great potential as a thriving, pace-setting town and I'm proud to be part of the force behind that." He looked out over the adoring faces of the town's high society. "There are good people here—the best! Your kind hearts and foresight are the backbone of the pride we share in our community. I left the town of my birth when I was only seventeen because I thought I wouldn't be accepted. Thank you for proving me wrong. No one should underestimate the democratic ideology and American values of Shadow Valley." He felt a curious tension moving through the crowd, saw eyebrows rise and mouths drop open. *It was time.*

He continued without a pause, "I'm pleased about your support of my efforts to restore Pebble Street to a place of pride. Your input and enthusiasm are exemplary, and brilliant not only from a commercial standpoint but from a historical one. It's a project close to the heart of this kid who spent his childhood on Pebble Street." He raised his glass and his voice. "So, a toast to the warm and gracious citizens of Shadow Valley. I thank you for welcoming me home."

A profound hush moved over the ballroom. Cody went on with his charade of assuming they had known all along who he was, expecting them to fall into the role he had dictated. What choice had he given them, after all?

The silence waned after a time. Dr. Jeff Calhoun took his cue and rushed to shake Cody's hand with gusto. Ben Engleson was right behind him, openly annoyed that the veterinarian had the gall to go first, before the mayor.

A bubble of gaiety bounced through the crowd. Cody watched with amusement. How shaken they were and how proud of themselves! His strategy had worked. Victory felt damn good.

Only one thing was missing. Ellen ought to be here. This was her victory, too. Without her at his side, he felt a poignant emptiness in his triumph.

IRIS WHITFIELD WAS maddeningly tenacious. She appeared repeatedly in Ellen's dreams, always in the front parlor of the mansion. Sometimes Cody was in the dream and sometimes he wasn't. Did it mean he was forgetting her? It was unnerving to know that he was likely dreaming the same dream at the same moment. But it was worse to think that at some point in time he would stop dreaming about her.

"What the devil do you want?" she asked the ghost. "It's too late for anyone to do anything—I did try." Iris would hate to have her house transformed into a hotel; she must be extremely distraught.

One evening a letter from Cody was in the mailbox when she came home from work. Heart jumping at the sight of his large handwriting, she ripped it open eagerly.

Dear Ellen,
I've been thinking of you, as always. Wanted to tell you the buyer of your mansion pulled out six weeks ago. Seems the house is so haunted, no workers would stay. I spoke with three of them personally. Stories were that some rooms were ice cold and there were strange smells and unpleasant noises and even things falling and breaking....

Ellen gasped. Accounts just like this were spread by Carolyn Meullar years ago. It had to be why the house had stood empty for so long. Iris had been angry when the Meullars lived there and she was angry now.

I've been appointed city manager. The project to restore Pebble Street went into high gear right after your house sold. Artists and retirees are already living there. Meredith finally spoke to me long enough to say she'd like to plead with you to have a Tarot reading in N.Y. for the sake of your long friendship. Saw her at the Ball and your dresses, too, which stole the show until my speech when I told them I came from Pebble Street. Quite a sensation. I wish you had been at my side. I love you and always will.

The words blurred on the page. A postscript mentioned a radio conference coming up in Denver. Cody's anger had dissolved and so had hers. When she fell into bed exhausted from the long day his words rang in her head. *The mansion hasn't sold after all.... It's too haunted....*

On Saturday she came home in a daze from an appointment with a Tarot reader. Four of the ten cards had been identical, including the Lovers and the Tower and the Fool— an almost-impossible phenomenon. The reading had been astoundingly like Meredith's, even to the point when the reader—a psychic in Hell's Kitchen—told her she was now in a location where she didn't belong.

Meredith hadn't lied to her. She had tried to say so and Ellen had been too hurt to listen. Shaking, she dialed Meredith's number but there was no answer.

Ellen couldn't hold back the tears. *What have I done? I was so defensive about my plans . . . so determined to be respected . . . so blinded by the snobbery of the town. . . .*

That night, Iris appeared in her dream not as a filmy apparition but as a young woman wearing her wedding dress. When she moved, a ghostlike mist rose up around her. Iris was beckoning. In a glow like moonlight, tears were gleaming on her cheeks.

Behind Iris, Cody appeared, wearing jeans and a T-shirt, his arms reaching out to her. "Ellen, come back to me. I love you."

17

Waking with a start, Ellen missed him desperately. The cold, dark room closed in around her like a cave. "Cody!" she cried aloud, knowing it was his dream, too. He wouldn't plead for her to return except in his sleep when his love reached across two thousand miles of darkness.

And Iris! She was pleading. How lovely she had been in her wedding gown—the gown that now lay on the shelf in Ellen's closet, still in its box tied with blue ribbon.

It was nearly six o'clock. Four in the morning in Colorado. Cody had just wakened from a dream of her. Ellen buried her face in her hands.

> *Morning sunlight, golden beams,*
> *Show me riches, show me dreams.*
> *Sunlight, shine a path for me*
> *Toward the place I'm meant to be.*

Carolyn would never be able to sell that haunted house, she thought. Iris would see to that. It served the family right for stealing it. It could be bought dirt cheap by anyone who wasn't afraid of the ghost—the person who was meant to live there! This was Iris's message! She, Ellen Montrose, was wanted by the house and its ghost. And by the man who loved her. And a dear friend who loved her and hadn't betrayed her, after all.

"Oh, God," she muttered. "I'm being pulled back! I'm wanted because no one belongs there but me. No wonder I'm not happy in New York."

After her shower, it wasn't her reflection that looked back from the misted mirror. Instead she saw the front parlor where Iris had been standing in the dream. Ellen felt energy drawing her into the mirror and a second later she was there in the parlor looking through the bay window at the rooftops of the town below. There were new drapes and a polished desk holding drawings of her fashion designs. On one side a gold brocade curtain hung on a round platform—a fitting room. Through an arch were cutting tables and two new sewing machines. A shock of excitement shot through her. Was it a dream? A creation of her conscious mind? Whatever it was, Ellen welcomed it with a wild yelp as the best idea she had ever had.

Didn't all the big-name designers work for themselves? How many designers lived and worked in a *mansion*?

Her heart pounded. Cody had tried to tell her that making a place for oneself is better than looking for a place to fit—and waiting for someone else to give you the breaks! He had done it—taken control, made his own opportunity. So could she! She could return a success, too. She could return to a mansion that was rightfully hers.

WHEN JENNIFER WAS ready to leave for the subway that morning, Ellen waved her on. "I'll be late," she said, fumbling with the telephone. "Something has come up."

Her roommate eyed her with curiosity, but asked nothing, only shrugged and buttoned her coat as she hurried out the door.

Denver information supplied her with a telephone number for Mountain Properties—the name she had seen countless times on the weathered sign outside the mansion. She got a recorded message. Damn. It was only six-thirty in the Denver area. She dialed Cody's number and received no answer. Why wouldn't he be there this time of day? Unless he had slept elsewhere. The thought sent a chill through her that quickly changed to heat. And fear.

An hour later someone at the radio station answered. "He's in Denver at a conference," the man said. "We expect him back on Monday. Do you want to leave a message?"

"No, I'll call back." Cody had mentioned that conference in his letter.

Eventually a live voice answered at Mountain Properties. Ellen summoned up her most powerful voice. "I'm inquiring about the Whitfield house in Shadow Valley—the one that has been for sale for three years. I understand the most recent buyer canceled because of unpleasant phenomena inside the house. I know someone who might be willing to take it off your hands for a small down payment."

She was, of course, talking about her life savings, minus plane tickets, padded with money earned in New York, added to the surprise thirty-five thousand dollars cash she got for Gramps's house because of Cody's Pebble Street project.

The realtor hesitated. Ellen could hear papers shuffling in the background. "Our contract with the owner will expire in two days. We don't plan to renew it."

"You sound discouraged. About that house, I couldn't blame you."

"It's been nothing but a headache," the agent admitted. "We've had to tell people about the . . . odd goings-on there but none have been prepared to deal with them."

Ellen wondered if her head was going to burst with excitement. In two days, she thought, a new realtor would be representing Carolyn—one not clued in on how haunted the mansion was, and that realtor would be harder to deal with.

So she must act immediately. "We'll need to move fast, then, if you want to earn your commission," she said.

The agent's voice picked up energy. "Do you want to look at the property?"

"I know the house." The vision came in full color before her. A magnificent office in a mansion . . . a *mansion! The mansion of her dreams!* Hired seamstresses—two or three—and buyers from all parts of the state . . . Ellen cleared her throat to prevent her voice from shaking. "Twenty thousand down and a guarantee not to rescind the agreement. The owner carries the loan at nine percent for thirty years with option to pay off the mortgage at any time and I move in immediately. This is my final offer."

"I think the owner will accept it," the agent replied with unsuppressed glee. "Now. Are you in Denver?"

"No, but I will be in a few hours. I'm calling from New York City. Can you have the papers drawn up right away?"

"Yes. Did you say New York?"

"I'll fax my signed offer immediately, along with the exact time I can be in your office tomorrow, after I've checked airline schedules. My name is Ellen Montrose."

The rightful heir to Whitfield. She had known she belonged there, even as a kid. Part of her had always known.

THE BUS RIDE FROM DENVER to Shadow Valley seemed to last forever. Sitting at the window, holding the box with Iris's wedding dress on her lap so it wouldn't be crushed in her suitcase, Ellen looked out at the snow-capped mountains. Fall foliage had been pinched away by frost, and a hint of winter was in the air. It had been summer when she left—only last summer. It seemed so long ago.

And yet New York already seemed so far away and so long ago. Ellen had given Jennifer her share of an extra month's rent and an invitation to visit Colorado.

Exhilaration built as the bus brought her closer to home. Her vision of the parlor transformed into her place of business was becoming more vivid as she filled in details—wallpaper, an antique love seat, a silver tea set for serving tea to her clients....

Cody was right—conquering was better than running!

Maybe it was fortunate that she couldn't reach him before she left New York. Better to do this on her own. And it would be a thrill to surprise him. *Surprise* was hardly the word; he would be astounded. And yet . . . hadn't he called her home in his dream?

THE SKY WAS WINTER GRAY, like his mood. Driving home from Denver along the solitary road, Cody couldn't get the dream out of his head. Ellen's face had brightened when she saw him. Sparkles from somewhere—perhaps the chandelier—shone in her soft blue eyes. She had reached back—tried to reach him, tried to touch him. For the two days since, he had been unable to shake off the intensity of that fleeting moment. *She had tried to reach him.*

She belonged with him. The ghost of her ancestor knew she belonged in the mansion that should be hers. Iris had been successful in preventing the sale of her house. With all the horror stories circulating, any offer would be snapped up by the Meullar heir.

Any offer! Cody's foot pressed harder on the gas pedal, and his hands gripped the steering wheel. Why the devil hadn't he thought of it before?

He had seen in his dreams the way the house should be. He had even thought his dreams predicted the future. If he were to buy the house, would Ellen come back? He tried to evaluate possibilities. If she didn't, he'd be stuck with an enormous dwelling inhabited by an angry ghost.

Still, a lot of prestige was involved. Whoever lived there would be considered Shadow Valley's nobility. No one else in town knew why the previous buyer had backed out, and he, as city manager, had been careful to keep the reason from getting around, because it would discourage other bidders. As far as the town knew, the buyer simply hadn't been able to afford the stately old mansion.

The truth was, even he might be able to afford it. As he drove, Cody began to work the idea over in his mind.

SHE FELT THE palpitations of her own heart, coming faster and harder as the road became familiar. She had taken a seat behind the driver because she didn't intend to ride all the way into town. She would tell him where to stop.

As the bus rounded a steep slope, she saw it. High and proud on its hilltop, sunlight reflecting in sparks from the glass of its windows was the house of her childhood dreams. The house of her lover's dreams. The house of her future dreams. The house of her destiny.

The bus came to a stop in front of the gate. As soon as it had pulled away, Ellen set down her things by the side of the road to button her coat against the early-winter chill. She rested her hand for a moment on the leaning, faded For Sale sign. It gave under her weight as if it had no further reason to stand. With a thrill and a little prayer of thanks, she let it fall facedown in the tall, dry grass. In minutes Ellen was walking up the weed-grown path to the front door—suitcase in one hand, the wedding dress in the other, and two sets of keys in her purse. She was home.

In the front parlor, she ran a finger through the dust of the sill and looked out to the town below. "All right, I'm home," she said to the ghost who was somewhere near. Sun was streaming in through the bay window of the room that would be her place of business in *her mansion*. By doing much of the work herself, she could afford to renovate the lower rooms first. It was a little scary thinking about the mortgage payments, but the demand for her clothes had already been established before she left. It would work. Cody had once said Shadow Valley now belonged to him. "It can be mine, too," she said aloud, almost singing. "It can be *ours!*"

CODY SLOWED HIS CAR to pull off in front of the mansion. The phone number of the Denver realtor would be on the For Sale sign. To his shock, the sign wasn't there. How could it not be? He'd seen it on his way out of town last Thursday. Had some buyer materialized over the weekend? During the drive he had convinced himself he had to have Whitfield mansion.

Maybe the sign just fell or some kids pushed it down. Cody parked in front of the gate and got out, intending to look for the sign. But his attention was drawn to the house instead. The front door was standing open.

In all the years he'd known the mansion, never had he seen the door open. Someone was here, and that someone more than likely was the latest buyer. *He had to know.*

Cody started up the steep path. Halfway up, he saw a silhouette appear on the front porch—a slim woman whose body language reminded him of Ellen. Hell, every pretty woman made him think of Ellen. The figure stood quite still, watching him climb toward the house. Then suddenly, the woman held out her arms.

His last dream flashed in front of him—her reaching to him. . . . *Ellen?*

"Ellen?" He started to run.

She didn't move, but stood steadfast and triumphant in the doorway of the house, arms outstretched.

"Ellen!" He stumbled forward, his heart in his throat, nearly tripping on the rough path that suddenly seemed to get longer and steeper with each step he took.

Then, at last, he was within the shadow of her smile. With a new surge of energy, he bolted up the steps and into her waiting arms.

For a full minute they held each other in the sound of winter wind in the high eaves and the open door scraping on its hinges.

Ellen breathed, "I am home, my darling."

He stepped back to look at her, holding tightly to her shoulders, afraid to let go. "Ellen? Is this . . . is this another dream?"

Her laughter came like a song. "Yes! Oh, yes! One to last a lifetime!" She took his hands in hers and gazed into his eyes, which were bluer than she had ever seen them, even against the backdrop of the graying winter sky. "Oh, my love . . ." she whispered. "Welcome to my dream!"

Epilogue

ON DECEMBER TWENTY-FOURTH Ellen walked into the room she still called "the parlor" carrying the treasured box tied with blue ribbon. It was early morning; her seamstress wouldn't arrive for another two hours. So there was time.

She glanced around the room as she always did, admiring the reality of it, the beauty of it. Her place of business, already gaining a reputation that reached far beyond the confines of Colorado. In the bay window sat a Christmas tree decorated in pink-and-silver balls and ribbons. A welcoming wreath was on the door.

She passed through an archway that led to the adjoining room, where she set the box down, carefully lifted out Iris's wedding gown, and spread it lovingly over the broad worktable. Its fabric was almost perfectly preserved and spotlessly clean, the linen lace formed in paisley-like designs unlike any she had ever seen. She guessed that the material—possibly the finished dress—had been imported from Ireland. It was as lovely as a gown she could design herself, elegant in its classic simplicity. The waist looked quite small...but then, so was hers.

With gentle reverence, Ellen stepped out of her velveteen robe and into a gown that had not been worn in a hundred years. It clung to her body possessively.

She turned to the three-way mirror and drew an astonished breath. Never had she looked more beautiful.

A movement in the shadows caught her eye. "Iris!" Ellen exclaimed. "It's a magical dress!"

The ghostly form fluttered and moved nearer.

"Then you approve of my wearing it! I knew you would."

"I also approve of your wearing it," Cody said from the doorway.

She turned. "Oh! I didn't hear you come in! Cody, don't look!"

He turned his back to her. "Honey, I already have looked. My heart is thundering at the sight. Why did you tell me you hadn't even begun designing your dress?"

"I haven't. This is Iris's. I hadn't even thought...until early this morning. I think she put the idea in my head. No, don't! Don't turn around."

"Why not?"

"Tradition, silly. Iris and I have just decided this is the one I'm going to wear."

Cody let out a whoop. "All *right*. That means we don't have to wait. We can do it today."

Ellen slowly, reluctantly, slipped out of the gown and drew on her robe. "Right."

"Honey, I'm serious. You have your dress, what more do we need?"

She laughed. "A preacher. Flowers. Champagne. Invitations. You can turn around now."

He did, scratching his head. "What invitations?"

She stared at him. "The invitations I assume you want to send out to the citizens of Shadow Valley."

"Me? Why would I want to share the most important day of my life with them?"

Ellen's eyes widened in surprise. Then she drew in a breath of delight. "And why would I?"

He grinned. "The tables have turned, my sweet. Cream rises to the top."

"And then everybody wants a taste of it." She giggled. "The so-called aristocrats of Shadow Valley will be devastated if they're not invited."

"They'll get over it. We'll have a reception sometime later. If we feel like it. If not, we won't." He took her hand. "This wedding is ours, my love. We have to please only ourselves."

She hugged him tightly and nodded, her excitement mounting. "Tomorrow's Christmas!"

CANDLES FLICKERED in the living room. Colored Christmas lights were strung along the staircase. Cody, dressed in his tuxedo, with Jeff Calhoun at his side and the minister behind him, waited impatiently, standing on one foot and then the other, during a piano rendition of "The Rose" by the artist-musician who had purchased Ellen's house on Pebble Street.

When the music changed to Rachmaninoff's Pagonini Rhapsody, Meredith walked proudly down the stairway wearing a red formal gown from Ellen's private collection, and carrying red roses.

Cody's eyes fixed on his bride as she appeared at the first landing of the stairs, white roses in her hands, a vision of beauty. She floated down to the sweet strains of the music, colored lights reflected on her gown. Ellen's eyes fixed on his, and she smiled through her misty veil.

Am I dreaming? he wondered. *Or is life more dazzling than a dream?*

From his stance beside the makeshift altar of candles and flowers, Cody focused on Ellen's smile. Nothing else was real. He felt his feet move, as if propelled by an unseen force, toward the bottom of the stairs, where he waited until his bride could reach his extended hand.

Ellen smiled down at him, remembering the first time his hand had moved toward her on this very stairway—the dream before destiny brought them together.

The Christmas lights blinked wildly at the instant their hands clasped. All the candles began to wave and flicker as if a breeze were passing through; and on the breeze the subtle scent of iris blossoms mixed with lilacs—their wedding gift from *her*.

Walking hand in hand those few final steps into their future, Ellen seized a long-allusive truth: The ghost had lured a ragged, barefoot child with dreams of splendor, knowing that when dreams are blessed in the spirit world, everything is possible.

"Everything *is* possible," Cody said, his thoughts receiving hers again. "Welcome home, my darling."

HARLEQUIN®

Temptation

Secret Fantasies

Do you have a secret fantasy?

Willow Evans does. But it involved independence and solitude at the Cape Cod house she'd inherited from her grandmother. Not being torn between two men...who look identical...neither of whom can really exist...who both want her. One man loves her...the other needs her. Discover a tale of impossible love by Lynn Michaels in #542 NIGHTWING, available in June 1995.

Everybody has a secret fantasy. And you'll find them all in Temptation's exciting new yearlong miniseries, Secret Fantasies. Beginning January 1995, one book each month focuses on the hero or heroine's innermost romantic desires....

SF-6

HARLEQUIN®

Don't miss these Harlequin favorites by some of our most
distinguished authors!
And now, you can receive a discount by ordering two or more titles!

HT #25607	PLAIN JANE'S MAN by Kristine Rolofson	$2.99 U.S./$3.50 CAN.	☐
HT #25616	THE BOUNTY HUNTER		
	by Vicki Lewis Thompson	$2.99 U.S./$3.50 CAN.	☐
HP #11674	THE CRUELLEST LIE by Susan Napier	$2.99 U.S./$3.50 CAN.	☐
HP #11699	ISLAND ENCHANTMENT by Robyn Donald	$2.99 U.S./$3.50 CAN.	☐
HR #03268	THE BAD PENNY by Susan Fox	$2.99	☐
HR #03303	BABY MAKES THREE by Emma Goldrick	$2.99	☐
HS #70570	REUNITED by Evelyn A. Crowe	$3.50	☐
HS #70611	ALESSANDRA & THE ARCHANGEL		
	by Judith Arnold	$3.50 U.S./$3.99 CAN.	☐
HI #22291	CRIMSON NIGHTMARE		
	by Patricia Rosemoor	$2.99 U.S./$3.50 CAN.	☐
HAR #16549	THE WEDDING GAMBLE by Muriel Jensen	$3.50 U.S./$3.99 CAN.	☐
HAR #16558	QUINN'S WAY by Rebecca Flanders	$3.50 U.S./$3.99 CAN.	☐
HH #28802	COUNTERFEIT LAIRD by Erin Yorke	$3.99	☐
HH #28824	A WARRIOR'S WAY by Margaret Moore	$3.99 U.S./$4.50 CAN.	☐

(limited quantities available on certain titles)

	AMOUNT	$
DEDUCT:	**10% DISCOUNT FOR 2+ BOOKS**	$
ADD:	**POSTAGE & HANDLING**	$
	($1.00 for one book, 50¢ for each additional)	
	APPLICABLE TAXES*	$
	TOTAL PAYABLE	$
	(check or money order—please do not send cash)	

To order, complete this form and send it, along with a check or money order for the
total above, payable to Harlequin Books, to: **In the U.S.:** 3010 Walden Avenue,
P.O. Box 9047, Buffalo, NY 14269-9047; **In Canada:** P.O. Box 613, Fort Erie, Ontario,
L2A 5X3.

Name: _____

Address: _____ City: _____

State/Prov.: _____ Zip/Postal Code: _____

*New York residents remit applicable sales taxes.
Canadian residents remit applicable GST and provincial taxes.

HBACK-AJ2

MOVE OVER, MELROSE PLACE!

HARLEQUIN® *Temptation®*

THREE GROOMS:
Case, Carter and Mike

TWO WORDS:
"We Don't!"

ONE MINISERIES:

GROOMS ON THE RUN

Starting in May 1995, Harlequin Temptation
brings you an exciting miniseries called

GROOMS ON THE RUN

Each book (and there'll be one a month for three
months!) features a sexy hero who's ready to say,
"I do!" but ends up saying, "I don't!"

Watch for these special Temptations:

In May, I WON'T! by Gina Wilkins #539
In June, JILT TRIP by Heather MacAllister #543
In July, NOT THIS GUY! by Glenda Sanders #547

Available wherever Harlequin books are sold.

If you are looking for more titles by

GINA WILKINS

Don't miss these fabulous stories by one of
Harlequin's most distinguished authors:

Harlequin Temptation®

#25492	TAKING A CHANCE ON LOVE	$2.99	☐
#25500	DESIGNS ON LOVE	$2.99	☐
#25558	RAFE'S ISLAND	$2.99	☐
#25586	JUST HER LUCK	$2.99	☐
#25621	UNDERCOVER BABY	$2.99 U.S.	☐
		$3.50 CAN.	☐

(limited quantities available on certain titles)

TOTAL AMOUNT	$
POSTAGE & HANDLING	$
($1.00 for one book, 50¢ for each additional)	
APPLICABLE TAXES*	$_____
TOTAL PAYABLE	$_____
(check or money order—please do not send cash)	

To order, complete this form and send it, along with a check or money order
for the total above, payable to Harlequin Books, to: In the U.S.: 3010 Walden
Avenue, P.O. Box 9047, Buffalo, NY 14269-9047; In Canada: P.O. Box 613,
Fort Erie, Ontario, L2A 5X3.

Name: _____

Address: _____ City: _____

State/Prov.: _____ Zip/Postal Code: _____

*New York residents remit applicable sales taxes.
 Canadian residents remit applicable GST and provincial taxes.   HGWBACK2

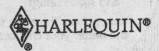

HARLEQUIN®

ANNOUNCING THE

FLYAWAY VACATION SWEEPSTAKES!

This month's destination:

Beautiful SAN FRANCISCO!

This month, as a special surprise, we're offering an exciting FREE VACATION!

Think how much fun it would be to visit San Francisco "on us"! You could ride cable cars, visit Chinatown, see the Golden Gate Bridge and dine in some of the finest restaurants in America!

The facing page contains two Entry Coupons (as does every book you received this shipment). Complete and return *all* the entry coupons; **the more times you enter, the better your chances of winning!**

Then keep your fingers crossed, because you'll find out by June 15, 1995 if you're the winner! If you are, here's what you'll get:

- Round-trip airfare for two to beautiful San Francisco!
- 4 days/3 nights at a first-class hotel!
- $500.00 pocket money for meals and sightseeing!

Remember: The more times you enter, the better your chances of winning!*

*NO PURCHASE OR OBLIGATION TO CONTINUE BEING A SUBSCRIBER NECESSARY TO ENTER. SEE REVERSE SIDE OR ANY ENTRY COUPON FOR ALTERNATIVE MEANS OF ENTRY.

VSF KAL

FLYAWAY VACATION
SWEEPSTAKES
<u>OFFICIAL ENTRY COUPON</u>

This entry must be received by: MAY 30, 1995
This month's winner will be notified by: JUNE 15, 1995
Trip must be taken between: JULY 30, 1995-JULY 30, 1996

YES, I want to win the San Francisco vacation for two. I understand the prize includes round-trip airfare, first-class hotel and $500.00 spending money. Please let me know if I'm the winner!

Name_____

Address _____ Apt. _____

City   State/Prov.   Zip/Postal Code

Account #_____

Return entry with invoice in reply envelope.

© 1995 HARLEQUIN ENTERPRISES LTD.   CSF KAL

FLYAWAY VACATION
SWEEPSTAKES
<u>OFFICIAL ENTRY COUPON</u>

This entry must be received by: MAY 30, 1995
This month's winner will be notified by: JUNE 15, 1995
Trip must be taken between: JULY 30, 1995-JULY 30, 1996

YES, I want to win the San Francisco vacation for two. I understand the prize includes round-trip airfare, first-class hotel and $500.00 spending money. Please let me know if I'm the winner!

Name_____

Address _____ Apt. _____

City   State/Prov.   Zip/Postal Code

Account #_____

Return entry with invoice in reply envelope.

© 1995 HARLEQUIN ENTERPRISES LTD.   CSF KAL

OFFICIAL RULES

FLYAWAY VACATION SWEEPSTAKES 3449

NO PURCHASE OR OBLIGATION NECESSARY

Three Harlequin Reader Service 1995 shipments will contain respectively, coupons for entry into three different prize drawings, one for a trip for two to San Francisco, another for a trip for two to Las Vegas and the third for a trip for two to Orlando, Florida. To enter any drawing using an Entry Coupon, simply complete and mail according to directions.

There is no obligation to continue using the Reader Service to enter and be eligible for any prize drawing. You may also enter any drawing by hand printing the words "Flyaway Vacation," your name and address on a 3"x5" card and the destination of the prize you wish that entry to be considered for (i.e., San Francisco trip, Las Vegas trip or Orlando trip). Send your 3"x5" entries via first-class mail (limit: one entry per envelope) to: Flyaway Vacation Sweepstakes 3449, c/o Prize Destination you wish that entry to be considered for, P.O. Box 1315, Buffalo, NY 14269-1315, USA or P.O. Box 610, Fort Erie, Ontario L2A 5X3, Canada.

To be eligible for the San Francisco trip, entries must be received by 5/30/95; for the Las Vegas trip, 7/30/95; and for the Orlando trip, 9/30/95.

Winners will be determined in random drawings conducted under the supervision of D.L. Blair, Inc., an independent judging organization whose decisions are final, from among all eligible entries received for that drawing. San Francisco trip prize includes round-trip airfare for two, 4-day/3-night weekend accommodations at a first-class hotel, and $500 in cash (trip must be taken between 7/30/95—7/30/96, approximate prize value—$3,500); Las Vegas trip includes round-trip airfare for two, 4-day/3-night weekend accommodations at a first-class hotel, and $500 in cash (trip must be taken between 9/30/95—9/30/96, approximate prize value—$3,500); Orlando trip includes round-trip airfare for two, 4-day/3-night weekend accommodations at a first-class hotel, and $500 in cash (trip must be taken between 11/30/95—11/30/96, approximate prize value—$3,500). All travelers must sign and return a Release of Liability prior to travel. Hotel accommodations and flights are subject to accommodation and schedule availability. Sweepstakes open to residents of the U.S. (except Puerto Rico) and Canada, 18 years of age or older. Employees and immediate family members of Harlequin Enterprises, Ltd., D.L. Blair, Inc., their affiliates, subsidiaries and all other agencies, entities and persons connected with the use, marketing or conduct of this sweepstakes are not eligible. Odds of winning a prize are dependent upon the number of eligible entries received for that drawing. Prize drawing and winner notification for each drawing will occur no later than 15 days after deadline for entry eligibility for that drawing. Limit: one prize to an individual, family or organization. All applicable laws and regulations apply. Sweepstakes offer void wherever prohibited by law. Any litigation within the province of Quebec respecting the conduct and awarding of the prizes in this sweepstakes must be submitted to the Regies des loteries et Courses du Quebec. In order to win a prize, residents of Canada will be required to correctly answer a time-limited arithmetical skill-testing question. Value of prizes are in U.S. currency.

Winners will be obligated to sign and return an Affidavit of Eligibility within 30 days of notification. In the event of noncompliance within this time period, prize may not be awarded. If any prize or prize notification is returned as undeliverable, that prize will not be awarded. By acceptance of a prize, winner consents to use of his/her name, photograph or other likeness for purposes of advertising, trade and promotion on behalf of Harlequin Enterprises, Ltd., without further compensation, unless prohibited by law.

For the names of prizewinners (available after 12/31/95), send a self-addressed, stamped envelope to: Flyaway Vacation Sweepstakes 3449 Winners, P.O. Box 4200, Blair, NE 68009.

RVC KAL